Beth Reekles is the author behind the 2018 Netflix smash hit movie, *The Kissing Booth*.

Beth first published *The Kissing Booth* on Wattpad in 2010, at age 15, accummulating almost 20 million reads before it was published by (Penguin) Random House in 2012, along with her other YA novels, *Rolling Dice* and *Out of Tune*. She has also published a short story with Accent Press called *Cwtch Me If You Can*.

Her work as an author saw her named as one of TIME's 16 Most Influential Teenagers in late 2013, and shortlisted for several awards, including the 2014 Queen of Teen awards.

She now works in IT while maintaining her career as an author, and runs a blog where she talks about life as a twenty-something and offers writing advice.

It Won't Be Christmas Without You is Beth's first adult fiction novel.

🐦 @Reekles
f www.facebook.com/Reekles/
📷 @authorbethreekles
www.authorbethreekles.com

It Won't Be Christmas Without You

Beth Reekles

OneMoreChapter

A division of HarperCollins*Publishers*
www.harpercollins.co.uk

One More Chapter an imprint of
HarperCollins*Publishers*
The News Building
1 London Bridge Street
London SE1 9GF

www.harpercollins.co.uk

This paperback edition 2019

First published in Great Britain in ebook format by
HarperCollins*Publishers* 2019

A catalogue record for this book
is available from the British Library

ISBN: 9780008354497

This novel is entirely a work of fiction.
The names, characters and incidents portrayed in it are
the work of the author's imagination. Any resemblance to
actual persons, living or dead, events or localities is
entirely coincidental.

Set in Birka by Palimpsest Book Production Ltd, Falkirk
Stirlingshire

Printed and bound in Great Britain by
CPI Group (UK) Ltd, Croydon CR0 4YY

For my sister, my tree-decorating and singalong partner. Love ya, Kat.

Twenty-five days to Christmas

Chapter 1

Eloise stared so hard into the camera that Cara tapped on her iPad screen, wondering if the connection had cut out. But then her twin blinked.

"What do you mean, you're *not coming home* for Christmas?"

Cara's face twisted. She knew Eloise would react like this. She'd braced herself for a screaming match, for tantrums, for tears and threats of never speaking to her again.

But she plastered on a big smile, noticing that her lipstick needed touching up. "I mean, technically, I will be. I'll just be there a bit ... later. It's not the end of the world!"

She really didn't see what the big deal was.

Eloise pursed her lips, eyes closing, head tilted down. It

was a look of grave disappointment, punctuated by a slow shake of the head. *She looks exactly like Mum when she does that*, Cara thought.

"That's not the point. Christmas is – well, it's Christmas. It's the whole holiday season. My tree's been up for weeks. And you're going to spend Christmas morning on a *bus*."

"It's not like there's much public transport running on Christmas Day. And it's the cheapest fare I could get," Cara admitted, before she could second-guess telling her sister that part. It wasn't as though she didn't spend a bloody fortune already, living in London. She rented one room in a five-bedroom house. Three bedrooms, technically – but who needed a dining room, or a loft, when you could convert them to bedrooms and rent them out at extortionate rates to desperate graduates trying to kick-start their careers?

Predictably, Eloise let out a snide bark of laughter, her phone screen tilting back towards the sky before she realigned it with her face. "Oh, of course. I hope you remembered to get yourself on Santa's Naughty List this year, Car, or you'll have to go buy that lump of coal to warm the house yourself."

Not for the first time in this conversation, Cara resisted the urge to roll her eyes. But her cheeks did colour, and her jaw worked furiously. So what if she was trying to save money? (And by save, she really meant 'not be broke'.) And so what if she wanted to go all out proving herself in her job to try and get a promotion in the New Year? Dave

2

Steers was leaving his editorial role in January and she knew for a *fact* they were going to recruit internally, and they were looking for someone with fresh, new ideas. Which could be her.

She'd worked so bloody hard over the past eighteen-odd months since graduating. Just four months into the job at the online lifestyle magazine and they'd run with one of *her* pitches to work with a handful of vloggers she'd suggested. Then, just a few months ago, they'd let her head up a campaign with a hugely popular mental health charity (an idea she'd pitched in the first place), with Dave Steers lending her a hand.

He knew she was gunning for his job. So did everyone else.

And if they wanted someone to fill his shoes while he was out of office for the week leading up to Christmas – well, she was more than happy to stuff on eight pairs of socks and fill those shoes.

Eloise was ranting at her while Cara tried to get a handle on her temper and not say something she regretted. Eloise was prattling on about her lack of Christmas spirit (Had she even worn her reindeer antlers yet this year? Her Santa hat, at least?), her workaholic attitude, the fact that they'd barely seen each other since that mini-break to Amsterdam in October their parents got them as a late birthday present, and what about their parents, and –

"And it's not like I'll be spending it with Josh this year," Eloise added, her tone quiet and sorry for herself.

Wow. She'd actually done it. She'd gone for the blackmail card. Guilting her twin with her own broken heart.

(Although, judging by the myriad of catastrophic Tinder conversations Eloise was always forwarding her screenshots of, Cara was willing to bet Eloise's heart was well on the mend.)

Cara arched an eyebrow at her sister. "Really? You want to play dirty? Fine. How about this: I can't afford to come home. I'm a poor graduate –"

"Content editorial assistant," Eloise interjected.

"– with a space heater to keep my shitty London loft room warm because the landlord won't fix the heating, and bugger all savings –"

"I did tell you I don't need a Christmas present this year. Especially one from Selfridges."

"Don't be stupid – you love that Bumble and bumble stuff. Anyway, that's not the point. I have to work. I need this promotion. People twice my age would kill for it. I'm lucky they're such a new company and they're willing to give me a chance like this. I'd have to work twenty years somewhere else for this kind of opportunity. If it means missing out on Dad's bacon sarnies and stockings on Christmas morning, well, that's fine by me."

Eloise gawped at her. "I'm going to pretend you didn't just say that."

She was going to miss Christmas morning at home, she knew, but she wasn't about to show Eloise any sign of weakness. The second her twin found a chink in her armour, she'd wear her down. And Eloise just didn't *get it*. She never had. Everything was always so easy for her.

Cara sighed, tapped her screen again to check the time. "Look, love, I've got to go. I need to freshen up before I go out."

"Is this another date with the dashing George?" Eloise's face finally brightened up, the sullen look disappearing in an instant at the inkling of gossip. "This will be – what, your fifth date now? Where's he taking you? Can it possibly top the couple's cooking class he took you to? Or, no, I take that back. Date number two was my favourite. Ice skating."

"Ice skating was a disaster. He sprained his wrist!"

"And you spent all night together in A&E laughing about it and getting to know each other. He *said* he only picked it because you said how much you like it. Although I'm still convinced he knew how bad he was going to be and only chose it as an excuse to hold your hand."

Cara grinned. She'd thought exactly the same thing from the second George had wobbled out onto the ice, grasping at the side and looking at her pleadingly until she'd taken his arm.

"They're playing *White Christmas* at some little cinema. We're getting dinner – probably just a Pizza Express or something, I reckon; he's not mentioned anything special – and then going to see the film."

A little of the sullen look returned, Eloise's brow furrowing. "Sure that's not too holly jolly for you?"

"Right. Thank you. I'm going now."

"Text me and let me know how the date goes!" Eloise shouted, leaning into the camera, as if she could force herself through it and be heard even if Cara hit the red hang-up button. Cara couldn't help but laugh at the beyond unflattering angle, giving her a great view of three chins and right up her sister's nostrils. "And use protection!"

"We're not sleeping together!" Cara protested, shouting just as loud, and then blushing quickly, having forgotten her housemates for a moment. At least two of them were home: she'd heard their footsteps clattering around the house.

"Well, excuse me. I thought you had a five-date rule."

Cara watched her ears turn red on the screen. "That's a personal guideline. Not a guarantee. And it's not like he's one of those guys who pushes for it. It's all totally PG right now. Which is just fine with me."

Eloise ignored her squirming, instead singing, "*You lurve him, you want to kiss him, you want to –*"

"I'll text you later."

London was pretty at Christmas, in its own way. There were no rolling hills that might get a dusting of snow, no roads lined with thick rows of trees that would droop heavy with frost. And the Tube – God, the Tube was a *nightmare* at the worst of times. And Oxford Street, for that matter.

But there was something uplifting about the solidarity

of the commuters and the tourists when Christmas tunes carried out of almost every pair of headphones and out of every shop front.

She'd been giddy with it last year. Eloise had come to visit for two days before they'd got the train back home together, and they'd spent an evening doing late-night Christmas shopping, taking dozens of photos and selfies for Instagram amidst all the lights and window displays on Oxford Street.

And it was still pretty, but this year it seemed to have lost a little of the magic.

Maybe it was because she wasn't going home for Christmas. Maybe it was because she and her housemates had all been too busy to sort out decorating the house. Maybe it was because she'd not even watched *Love Actually* yet.

Or maybe Eloise was right. Maybe she was turning into Scrooge.

Although she was sure Scrooge wouldn't have minded a free glass of prosecco on a Christmas voucher offer at Prezzo. She grinned at George as they clinked glasses over their pizzas.

(And damn if he didn't have the cutest smile. Those dimples would make anybody swoon.)

He worked in finance, for some big firm she'd seen at all the career fairs at uni. He was two years older than her, and she'd met him through one of her housemates. (So old school, Eloise had joked, promptly regaling her sister with another story of a disastrous date with some guy she'd met through Facebook.)

They'd been seeing each other, for want of a better term, for the past month. They both worked a lot, totally threw themselves into their jobs and loved it, and they both understood when the other wanted to postpone a date to just catch up on some sleep. Or stay late at the office.

Maybe they were a perfect match.

She never really thought of herself as a hopeless romantic, but Cara really wanted that to be the case. She'd never met anyone who made her believe in the concept of Mr Right until she'd met George.

There *was* that guy she'd dated briefly for three months in the spring. She'd known him from school and seen online he was working in the city, and they'd chatted online for a while before agreeing to meet. He hadn't been able to handle her working so much, and Cara had shrugged him off like a cold. She didn't need that kind of negativity around her.

But George – George was sweet. George used online voucher codes to nab them discounted pizza and free prosecco, a bargain-hunter after her own heart. George was clean-shaven with sweeping, always-immaculate blond hair, and she'd yet to see him without his Barbour jacket. He was the kind of guy she'd like to take home to her parents. (At some point. Maybe after date number eleven. If she ever had a weekend where she wasn't so exhausted or busy she could go back home to visit.)

And he was beyond easy to talk to. There was always something to talk about with him. And he was funny.

It was almost a shame she wasn't going home for Christmas. Maybe she'd have asked him to come visit, so she could introduce him to her parents.

Calm down, idiot, she told herself, getting carried away with her daydreams as George told her about his office's upcoming Christmas party, reliving anecdotes from last year's. *You've gone on five dates with the guy, counting this one. And texting him every day doesn't really count. You don't even know if he sees you as his girlfriend yet.*

Eloise would've called her a cotton-headed ninny-muggins.

But then, Eloise quoted Christmas films all year-round. Eloise would have mince pies at Easter if she had her way.

Almost as if he could read her mind, George segued from his absurdly drunk boss at last year's do to, "But I haven't even asked you yet – what are your plans for Christmas? When are you off home to the family?"

She didn't beat around the bush this time, like she had when she'd discussed it with Eloise. She just smiled, laughed breezily, and lifted her prosecco glass. "Oh, I'm not. Well, not until Christmas afternoon. I'm working through Christmas Eve."

George's head tilted to the side. "Is this to do with Dave's job?"

She nodded, grateful he didn't question her Christmas

spirit. This was why she liked George so much. He got it. "Yeah. I need to show them I'm serious if I want to be in with a real chance."

"That makes sense. And I bet you'll actually get peace and quiet going home Christmas Day. The trains'll be mad the couple of days before, with everyone trying to get home."

Cara's eyes widened, and she gestured a little too enthusiastically with her glass, almost sloshing prosecco everywhere. George smiled at it, eyes twinkling as they crinkled at the corners. "Exactly! This is what I mean! And it's like, *so* much cheaper – but according to Eloise I'm just being Scrooge. I'm not, right?"

"Absolutely not! I'm staying in the city over the holidays completely. All my mates will be around for New Year's, and I've got so much work to try and get through – year end deadlines, you know. My dad and step-mum said they'd like to get some winter sun, so I told them to go ahead. Might as well, eh?"

Okay, now maybe that was a step too far. "You told your parents to go away for Christmas? You won't see them at all?"

"They're going to come visit in the New Year. I've got a few days off. I'll take them to see a show; they always like that." He tore a pizza crust in half, concentrating on it for a moment before looking up at her through his fair eyelashes. "You could come with us, if you like. If that's not too presumptuous. I've –" He cut off with a laugh, blushing. "I've told them all about you. Is that weird? I know we've only had a few dates but ..."

"Oh, my God, no, I've done exactly the same thing with my parents about you!" Maybe the prosecco had made her bold, or maybe she was just excited to hear he was as keen on her as she was on him. Cara grinned at how relieved he looked to hear it.

They finished up their meal and walked hand-in-hand to the cinema around the corner, and Cara thought the lights all looked a little more magical already.

She wasn't being a Scrooge. Christmas in London was already looking up.

Twenty days to Christmas

Chapter 2

"Y ou need a hand with that?"

Eloise huffed, turning to look over her shoulder at Number 3, who was bundled up in a pea coat, woolly scarf and beanie hat, bracing himself for the cold. He smirked at her, and she doubted the offer was a serious one.

Jamie Darcy, her neighbour, put the *arsey* in Darcy.

And right now he looked more than a little miffed that she was blocking the stairs, jangling his car keys from the end of one of his leather-gloved fingers.

"I'm fine," she snapped, breathing a little heavily. She was sweating inside her coat. The bloody tree wouldn't fit in her Polo, and she'd had to take the bus. Which meant carrying the eight-foot thing up the hill to the block of

13

flats, earning glares whenever a rogue pine needle jabbed someone who got too near. The single flight of stairs up to her front door was the real struggle, though.

Jamie stepped to one side, watching her struggle to drag it up another step. "Isn't that a bit too big for the flat?"

He would know: the flats on this street were all identical. Six in a building, two per floor, and seven block-like buildings of them curving around the street. And while they were reasonably spacious, they probably wouldn't fit an eight-foot tree easily.

"It's not for my flat." God, she really had to get to those cross-fit classes more. Or, like, at all. "It's for the school."

"Right. And you're stuck with it because ...?"

"Because I offered to pick it up. Because some of us like to do nice things for other people at Christmas." And because when the head had asked her to get it, she couldn't exactly turn around and say no, not when she'd made such a big deal out of how much she loved Christmas, getting stuck into the nativity and setting up lunchtime craft classes with the kids to make their own decorations, or decorate Christmas biscuits. Plus, she was the one who'd found a real Christmas tree within budget. She'd kind of made it her responsibility.

"Alright, hint taken. Mind out the way."

Before she could object, he brushed past her. Apparently immune to the pine needles poking through the netting, he hoisted it up, wrapping his arms around it.

Eloise tripped out of the way, fumbling in her coat

pocket for her keys and unlocking the door so Jamie could drop it just inside the hallway. He looked around, curious, taking in the wooden white-painted snowflakes hung on red string from the ceiling, the tinsel around the canvas on the wall, the reams of wrapping paper spilling out of a box she'd left out in the hallway.

"It's like an elf threw up in here."

"I went for an understated look this year," she dead-panned, although it wasn't a lie. Last year she'd tacked up those shiny concertina things all over the place. Josh had hated them though, so she'd donated them to the school after a week of him complaining.

Of course, she could have whatever she liked in the flat this year.

The thought still kind of stung.

"Yeah, looks like it."

"Thanks for the help," she said a little brusquely, by way of telling him to stop trying to see the rest of her flat and leave now, please.

Jamie had been in the building a couple of months before she'd moved in, in August last year, and even though they'd been polite enough to each other, he always gave the impression he had somewhere better to be. She'd never taken much of a liking to him – and Eloise prided herself on being someone who made an effort to get on with *everyone*. (She'd had to when Cara had always been such a social butterfly at school, the one who everyone wanted as a friend.)

"No problem. But, um, quick question – how exactly are you planning on getting that to the school? Or even back downstairs?"

"Someone's giving me a lift. Someone with a big enough car to fit this tree. They'll give me a hand."

Jamie nodded, and gave her a cursory smile as he stepped back out. "Fair enough. See you."

"Yeah, see you. Thanks again." And she shut the door behind him.

The stress of the tree finally off her shoulders, she sagged against the door, sighing out heavily before kicking off her boots and tossing her coat and bag onto the chair she left near the door purposely for that. She'd hang the coat up later.

She flicked the kettle on and padded into the living room to put the TV on, flipping through the channels and settling on Film4. It was one of the *Fast & Furious* movies – not as festive as she'd have liked, but one she didn't mind joining partway through.

The sound of the kettle boiling pulled her back to the kitchen, but not before she snapped on the fairy lights. She'd laid a string of them on the cabinet the TV sat on, and of course there were the ones on her own Christmas tree. It was a five-foot, slightly sparse-looking thing, but once she'd smothered it in tinsel and baubles and multi-coloured fairy lights (and, of course, some Cadbury tree chocolates) it was perfect.

And a sit-down with a movie for an hour was exactly

what she needed, completed with a mince pie and cuppa in her snowman mug. Perfect.

Perfection was interrupted in the next ad break though, with the sound of an incoming FaceTime.

Eloise sighed, licked the last mince pie crumbs off her finger and set down the plate on the sofa before reaching for her phone and swiping the screen open. "Hi, Mum."

She was greeted by the sound of *Mele Kalikimaka* playing from somewhere, and a pair of snowman deely boppers wobbled on her mum's head.

"Why are you wearing sunglasses?" she asked, before her mum had chance to say hello.

"Oh, darling! I thought it was dark!" This was punctuated by a giddy laugh that made Eloise wonder if her parents had cracked the Christmas Baileys open a little early. Her mum swept the sunglasses off her face. "We've got news! Your dad's just on FaceTime to Cara to tell her now. Actually, it was all her idea. Sort of. That boyfriend of hers, George. He gave us the idea."

"*What* are you talking about?"

"We've booked a holiday!"

Eloise caught sight of herself in the little window on her phone: one eye squinted shut, brow furrowed, top lip pulled up on one side in utter confusion. "Um, okay. That's nice, Mum."

"For Christmas!"

Eloise practically heard Santa's sleigh crash-landing to Earth.

Her mum, oblivious, carried on, talking a mile a minute, eyes glazed and mouth in a beaming smile. "See, Cara told us all about how George's parents have booked a last-minute holiday to get some winter sun for a week over Christmas, so we had a look and oh, sweetheart, you wouldn't believe the deal we got! A week in Tenerife, all inclusive! Absolute bargain! We fly out on the twenty-third, so we'll be back just in time for New Year. I'd hate to miss Sandra's New Year's do down the pub. They put on a cracking night."

Oh, yeah, Eloise thought bitterly, fighting hard not to say it out loud. *God forbid you miss the New Year's do at the local pub, but sure, skip Christmas; that's not a big deal.* It wasn't like Cara hadn't already mucked things up by deciding to travel home on Christmas Day instead of a few days earlier. It wasn't like she wasn't already kind of dreading her first Christmas in *years* without Josh and looking forward to a few days with her family more than ever. Especially with Cara. It felt like forever since they'd really hung out or spent any time together.

"I'm so glad I've been going to those fitness classes with the girls to shed a few pounds ready for Christmas. I don't know where I would've got a swimming costume and sundresses at this time of year if I didn't still fit into them! And your dad's bought one of those Hawaiian shirts, a bright yellow one with big pink flowers on. Looks bloody ridiculous, of course, but there was no stopping him!"

There's no stopping you going, either. Clearly.

"So ..." Eloise swallowed the lump in her throat. Vin Diesel was back on the TV, and she reached for the remote to mute it. "So you're going on holiday for Christmas. And Cara's not coming home. So I'm – I'm spending Christmas all on my own."

"Oh, no, don't be silly! Of course you can still come home, and Cara will be here – just not first thing in the morning. And she's said she can work from home for a day or so if she has to. And you could always go see your aunt and uncle and your cousins."

The aunt and uncle and cousins who lived over an hour's drive from home, who she didn't actually talk to all that much, and only saw a few times a year since she'd gone off to uni. And who didn't even cook a *turkey* on Christmas Day, because 'it was too much hassle'.

Her mum was still going on: about the hotel (four and a half stars on TripAdvisor, you know) and the one utterly scathing review (but of course it was probably a one-off) and how close they were to the beach, and –

And Eloise could see how excited her mum was. Her dad's voice was faint, somewhere in the background under what was now Michael Bublé's *Holly Jolly Christmas*, chattering away to Cara to tell her exactly the same news. He was just as excited.

And why shouldn't they be? They loved their sunny holidays in the Mediterranean. Of *course* they'd love a bit of winter sun for a change.

It wasn't their fault she didn't like to let on how homesick she got or how lonely she could be here.

So she plastered on a smile, asked her mum all the right questions, pretended that this was fine – they'd FaceTime from the beach! Her parents would have the best time! Of course Eloise didn't mind! They'd send each other pictures of their Christmas dinner! Ha ha!

(God, Christmas dinner – that was always her dad's domain ... What the hell would they do? Would Cara expect her to do it all? They couldn't *not* have a roast dinner on Christmas Day.)

It was all Cara's fault. Cara and that bloody guy she was seeing, George. Eloise had only heard wonderful things about perfect, dashing, handsome George so far, but this made her kind of hate him. He'd ruined Christmas.

Cara had sort of ruined Christmas when she'd phoned a few days ago, to say she wouldn't be there the whole day. But Eloise could just about live with that. It wouldn't be great, but they'd still have most of the day, and it wasn't like she'd be off to Josh's in the evening like she had the last several Christmases.

She could live with Cara bailing on Christmas morning. But this?

Christmas was the best time of year. For Eloise, it properly started as early as November. She'd been so excited about going back home and spending a few days with her family, watching the usual suspects on DVD, playing games, eating too much ...

And now she'd be waking up on Christmas Day all alone. In a big, empty house.

Alone at Christmas.

Did it get much worse than that?

Eighteen days to Christmas

Chapter 3

"**Y**ou coming?"

"Huh?"

Jen rolled her eyes, absently tapping her card wallet on the dividing wall around Cara's desk. "Starbucks. I literally just explained. You said you were listening."

"Sorry." Cara stared intently at her screen, eyes scanning the email once more, deleting one more exclamation mark before she hit send. She looked up at Jen again. "Sorry. I swear I'm listening this time."

"Starbucks time. Are you coming?" Cara's eyes flicked towards Dave's office, and she barely opened her mouth before Jen added, "Dave was the one who asked if anybody else wanted to go out and grab a Christmas coffee in the first place."

"I don't know. I've just got so much to get through for next week's last-minute gifts campaign ..." As if on cue, an email from some boutique candle company from North Wales pinged into her inbox. Promptly followed by a reply from the high street retailer they were still hoping to pin down. "I'm just ..."

"Oh my God," Jen sighed, exasperated but half-laughing, "don't bother. You'll just have your nose in your phone. What shall I bring you back?"

Jen had started her role in the PR team the same week as Cara had joined the company. Despite the four-year age difference, they'd clicked instantly. It hadn't been long before their joint coffee breaks and lunches turned into after-work drinks and weekend wanders around the shops. Jen was a brilliant friend, especially at times like this, when she understood how much Cara had on her plate.

The company – Klikit – had been around for maybe four years now, but it had only really started taking off about a year ago, hitting the front page of the App Store, their followers spiking on Twitter until they were real competitors, a real household name. They still had a way to go, and everyone in the office worked hard to make it happen – and Cara loved it. She thrived on the pressure, the new challenges that hit her email inbox every day. She loved the team, the platform, the work, all of it.

But she also loved a good Christmassy coffee.

"Toffee nut. With cream. Unless you end up at Costa instead, then I'll have the gingerbread latte. Ooh, and grab me a muffin while you're there? Something festive-flavoured. I don't care what. So long as it's not a mince pie. I might vomit if I have to see another mince pie."

People had been bringing boxes of them into the office for about a month now.

Eloise would have loved it. And Cara had at first – but there were only so many mince pies a person could eat. What was she – Father Christmas?

"Gotcha." Jen waggled her fingers as a few others wandered over, already wrapped in coats and ready to go. "We'll see you in, like, an hour."

Cara waved them all off as they passed by her desk and stuck her head back into her computer, sucked into a world of draft posts and stock images and emails, barely looking up until the smell of toffee nut slid under her nose.

"Love ya."

"You're welcome," Jen sang back. Cara looked up long enough to roll her neck, reviving the muscles there, and taking a long sip of her still-steaming hot latte. Heaven. This was liquid Christmas. Sod eggnog: this was the real magic, right here.

Jen was already chattering away, telling her about the latest office gossip that had surfaced, and Cara gave herself ten minutes to indulge in it. (Because damn, was Molly in Finance really hooking up with Patrick from IT? Didn't she have a boyfriend, or something?)

Eventually, Jen wandered back to her desk and Cara shifted back into full-on work mode.

When six o'clock hit and she broke off another bit of muffin to munch on, Dave passed by her desk.

"Dude," he said, "go home."

He called everyone dude. He even called the cleaning lady dude.

"I will, in a minute. I've just ..." *Ping.* Who the hell was even still working at six o'clock to reply to her emails now? Weren't office hours over?

Cara started replying.

Dave laughed, leaning against the desk next to her. "You don't have to keep working twelve hours a day, you know. You're already a shoo-in. You work twice as hard as anyone here. You already do half of my job for me."

Cara dragged her face away from the screen, and then her eyes a moment later. She smiled and said, "I swear, I'll go home as soon as I've sorted this. I just want to make sure it's done before I head off."

What she didn't add was that she *did* have to keep working like this, to prove herself. That was how she'd always been, though, in fairness, it wasn't so much to do with the company as it was her. But, even so, there were people who'd been here since Klikit started who would be interested in Dave's job. She was twenty-two and had been here only eighteen months. It seemed like way too soon to be looking for a promotion. So yes, she did have to work like this.

If she didn't get the promotion, nobody could say it was because she didn't work hard enough. Besides, she loved her job. It didn't feel so awful working this much when she enjoyed what she was doing.

Dave shook his head, laughing softly. "Alright, but seriously – get yourself home." He nodded at the screen. "That'll still be there in the morning. And hey – make sure you turn your phone off at the Christmas party next week. We can't have you working all night. This place won't fall apart if you take a break, you know."

She laughed. "Roger that, boss."

It was eight o'clock before she walked through the door at home. It was pitch dark outside, but the house was warm (for a change) and smelled like enchiladas.

With all of her housemates working such different jobs (a bar manager, someone in digital marketing for a chain of clubs, one girl in HR for a high-street fashion brand, and another guy working as a journalist), they didn't always get to spend a lot of time together. And *some* people (not that she was naming names, but it was totally Henry) never replaced the toilet roll when they used the last of it.

But times like this – when they made more than enough food and told her there were leftovers in the fridge – she loved them dearly.

Cara dumped her backpack near the door and tossed her coat onto the peg in the hallway.

"There's food in the fridge!" shouted one of her housemates, Jamilla, from the living room. "Elliot made enchiladas."

"Thanks!" Cara called back, heading straight for the kitchen now and digging the leftovers out of the fridge. Ooh, and they'd left some salad too. Absolute angels.

The idea of living with four total strangers had been terrifying at first, for Cara. A new city *and* a new job? Sure, that was exciting. But sharing a house with four totally random people?

A couple of people she knew from uni had done it too, and she'd heard a few horror stories of nightmare housemates or awful landlords, so she had to count her blessings: her housemates were so easy to get on with. And they did things like cook enough food for everyone and keep the house clean, which was a huge step up from some people she'd lived with at university.

Enchiladas reheated, Cara headed into the living room, where she could hear some of her housemates talking over the TV.

"Alright, Cara?" Elliot said, glancing up from his own plate of food. Jamilla was there too, stretched across the other sofa flicking through a magazine. While Cara ate, the three of them swapped stories about their days until Cara's phone buzzed.

She'd not checked her phone since she'd left work and noticed she had a few notifications. A text from Eloise. A photo from her mum in their family group WhatsApp, of the matching *#Elfie* T-shirts she and Cara's dad had bought to take on holiday. A missed call and now a text from George.

28

Her face lit up: it must've done, because Jamilla promptly said, "Oo-ooh, let me guess. A text from the famous George."

"Maybe."

"He's a keeper, C, I swear to God," Elliot pitched in. "How many guys do you think spend their lunch break coming to your office just to bring you your favourite Starbucks?"

"That was one time." But it had been a really nice surprise yesterday: he'd had to cancel their date the night before at short notice and wanted to make up for it, even though she'd understood.

"Go on, abandon your friends; call lover boy back," Jamilla told her, grinning. "If you don't, I will."

Cara stuck her tongue out, collecting the empty mugs, cereal bowl and her own plate to take to the kitchen. She called George back, sticking the phone on speaker as she loaded the things into the half-full dishwasher.

George answered almost straight away. "Hey! How are you? Are you back from work now?"

"Yeah. Sorry I missed your call; it must've been when I was on the Tube. I've only just had tea."

"I'm visiting a mate about two stops from you – is it alright if I pop in tonight? If you're not too tired? I'd love to see you."

"Oh! Um, sure. Yeah, absolutely!" She cringed, gritting her teeth. Did she sound too keen? Too late now. "Text me when you're here; I'll come down and let you in."

She'd been looking forward to cuddling up under the duvet with one of the Hallmark Christmas movies on Netflix. Eloise had been messaging her recommendations and out-of-five-stars reviews all week. But she could pass that up to see her (sort-of) boyfriend.

She hoped he was her boyfriend.

God, she hated this whole label thing. Talking to each other, seeing each other, dating – why were there so many labels for it now? Why was it so bloody intimidating to just *ask* him if they were a couple?

She hadn't even wondered about it too much until she'd gone to buy him a Christmas card the other day – and realised maybe he'd be freaked out if she got him a boyfriend card. Or disappointed to get one that didn't say 'boyfriend'.

"I have to ask you something."

"Sounds serious." Cara twisted towards him. They were lying side by side on her bed under about three blankets, her laptop propped on George's knees with the credits of *Jingle All The Way* rolling.

"Is it too weird if I get you a present? For Christmas? I mean, I know I said the other week about you meeting my parents, but you can back out of that easy with some excuse about work and I wouldn't even know if you made it up or not."

Cara wondered who'd made him so cynical about relationships.

She'd also never been so relieved to find a guy who didn't mind tackling head-on the kind of questions she worried about herself.

"I'll outdo you on the weird serious question front," she said, propping herself up on one elbow. "Do I get to call you my boyfriend yet, or do we have to go through some weird phase of casual-yet-exclusive dating for a few more weeks before that?"

George laughed so warmly that she felt she already knew the answer. It gave her the same warm, fuzzy feeling in her stomach as she got whenever she watched *Love Actually*.

"I think we can skip that phase, don't you?"

"Skip it all," she deadpanned, waving a hand. "I'll expect a Tiffany ring for Christmas. June wedding. Kids by October."

"Steady on. It'll have to be a winter wedding. My step-mum will murder me if she's stuffed up with hay fever in all the wedding photos. You think your parents would mind a child out of wedlock?"

"Hmm, not sure. Or we could just elope."

"Las Vegas at New Year? Elvis can officiate."

"Sounds like a plan to me."

"Well, thank you very much, little lady, thank you very much," he said, in possibly the worst impression of Elvis she'd ever heard.

Cara broke into peals of laughter and George set the laptop safely to one side before rolling on top of her, propped up on his elbows and kissing her softly. Cara sighed, leaning up into it, smiling against his lips.

"I can't stay too late," he murmured, breaking away with a groan and pushing his forehead against her cheek. "Early start."

"Or you could just ... stay here." Cara felt herself blushing furiously. Even though they'd had sex (after date number six) they hadn't *actually* spent the night with each other. "I've got a spare toothbrush in a drawer."

George laughed. "Well, that was the deal breaker."

Clearly she'd done something right to get on Santa's Good List this year, because George was utterly perfect.

Fourteen days till Christmas

Chapter 4

She could do this. Only a few more days of school to go until they broke up for the holidays, and then – then she'd never have to go through another run of that bloody nativity again.

If Eloise had to hear *Away in a Manger* or *Don't Stop Me Now* again any time soon, she'd scream. They'd been playing on a constant loop all day while the children did full run-throughs. And much as Eloise loved seeing them so happy and so full of Christmas spirit, it was driving her a little nuts.

Pouring herself a generous glass of white wine, she'd never been so glad to sink into her sofa. She FaceTimed Cara, but the call cut off before it was answered and she got a text instead.

Still in work and going straight to meet George. I'll try to call you later xxx

PS How's the nativity going? On the vino yet?

Eloise couldn't help but feel disappointed, even as she typed out upbeat replies filled with emojis. It was gone six and she knew from Cara's Instagrammed coffee at 7.32 a.m. that morning that she'd been in work early.

At school and at uni, Eloise always thought they'd both worked as hard as each other. They'd both fallen in love with Birmingham, and had lived in the same halls and house share throughout their degrees. Eloise wasn't finding it hard to be away from Cara lately so much as she found it hard to just *talk* to her sister. Especially with all this promotion stuff going on. Cara worked too bloody hard.

So bloody hard she was even skipping Christmas and had encouraged their parents to do the same.

Eloise fired off the last few wine glass emojis to Cara and a Snapchat to match, then set her phone aside. "Humbug," she muttered.

And giggled. A half-glass of wine and she was already tipsy. She probably should've eaten something before opening the bottle.

By the time she'd finished her glass, a movie had started on one of the TV channels and she left it to play, snuggling into her woolly cardigan and snapping off the lamp beside her. The Christmas tree and the fairy lights were all on, and she'd lit a cinnamon sugar-scented candle, so the room was lit with a warm, festive glow.

Bliss.

Lonely bliss, but still some kind of bliss.

Wryly, she thought this was probably more festive than Christmas morning would be.

Cara's fault.

She'd barely settled in with the movie when there was a knock on her door.

Eloise sat up, muted the TV. Cocked her head and listened.

Another knock. Definitely her door.

She didn't understand who it would be. Someone in the block, surely. You had to have a key to get into the building, or a special code for the intercom. If someone wanted to actually, physically knock her door, they had to get into the building first.

Another knock, this one harder, more insistent.

Eloise clambered up from the sofa, staggering a little as the wine hit her, and giggling while she steadied herself. Once she got to the door (which took at least three times as long as usual) she peered through the peep-hole.

Jamie knocked again, hammering his fist against the door. "I saw your lights on from outside, Eloise. I can hear you moving around."

She undid the chain and opened the door. She lifted her chin primly, pursing her lips. "Can I help you?"

She hiccupped.

Giggled again, pressing a hand to her mouth. Her whole face felt warm.

Jamie raised an eyebrow, but then went back to looking sullen and moody. Brooding, maybe. *Brooding* was a word that suited him. In a very Jon Snow-esque way. And ooh, he was wearing glasses. She'd never seen him in glasses before. Rectangular, black frames. They suited him. A lot. He cleared his throat, distracting her from looking at him. (And she really was only *looking*, definitely not staring. Not at all.) "I, um, I need a favour."

"Do you need more wrapping paper?"

He'd knocked on her door two days ago, needing paper to wrap a Secret Santa gift for someone in work. He'd laughed at her collection of ribbons and bows and tags, but taken some anyway, smirking when she told him he'd picked the wrong ones to match the paper.

"No. I, um ..." Jamie cleared his throat and stood up straighter, which was when she realised he'd been slouching. He was so much taller than her when he didn't slouch, and she wasn't in her usual heeled boots. His cheeks reddened. "I locked myself out. I went to take the recycling out and just ... I forgot my keys. Obviously I can get into the building, but ... not my flat. I tried the estate agent for a spare key, but they're shut till the morning. I know this is a really weird favour to ask, but ..."

"You can stay here," Eloise said, before he could stammer and drag it out any more. God, he was making it painful. Like this was more trouble for him than it would be for her. *Prick*, she thought, but smiled politely. "It's not a problem. Have you eaten yet? I might order some pizza. I'm *starving*."

"I could eat."

Eloise stepped aside, waving a hand grandly to admit him into the flat. She closed the door after him, and was pleased that he made use of the shoe rack without her even having to ask.

Jamie followed her into the living room, perching on the other end of the sofa. He looked awkward and out of place. He must've felt it too, because he ran a hand back and forth through his hair, mussing it up, cleaned his glasses on his T-shirt, rubbed his jaw.

Had he always looked this cute?

Maybe it was the glasses. Or the messy hair.

He might be too long for the sofa, Eloise wondered. But she could hardly offer him the bed. That was where she was sleeping.

He pointed at the TV and she followed his finger while she picked her phone up from where it had fallen on the floor earlier. She checked it for notifications, even though she knew there would be none. "Good movie."

"Is it? I've not seen it before."

She couldn't even remember what it was called. Just that it was some movie with Daniel Radcliffe, about magic, and not *Harry Potter*. Mark Ruffalo was currently on screen.

Eloise loaded the Dominos app, picking a two-pizza

deal and choosing one for herself before handing the phone to Jamie to pick what he wanted.

"I'll pay you back tomorrow, when I manage to get into my flat."

She waved him off as she tapped in the credit card details she knew off by heart. A side-effect of a lot of online shopping at university and a lack of ability to budget. "Don't worry about it, honestly. You want some wine? Tea? I've got some coffee, but it's only decaf. Um ... there's some lemonade too. Or orange juice. Or –"

"Tea would be nice. I'll make it, though, don't worry. Do you want one?"

"Um." Did people actually do this? Make themselves at home in someone else's kitchen? She'd only ever seen that in movies before. Was it arrogance, or was he being polite? It was hard to tell. She'd have opted for some more wine if she'd been on her own, but sobering up seemed like a better idea now she had company. "Yeah, go on then."

She half-watched the movie while she listened to him fill her kettle, look through a couple of drawers for the teaspoons, take mugs off the mug tree and open her tin labelled, unambiguously, TEA.

She wanted to text Cara. She wanted to call her and have a whispered conversation to say her arsey neighbour was spending the night at her flat. But Cara would be with George now, and she didn't want to disturb them.

Jamie handed her the tea. "Sorry – I forgot to ask if you

take sugar. But, given that there's a canister of tea bags out and no sugar, I'm guessing not."

Eloise shook her head. Her fringe was falling out of its hairpin, tucked off her face. "Nope. Thanks."

"No – thank *you*. Honestly. I really appreciate this. I know it's – I know I'm not exactly neighbourly, so I appreciate this."

Aww. That might be the first genuinely nice thing he'd ever said to her.

"It's no problem. Although, honestly, I'm a little worried you're too tall for the sofa. And I don't have an airbed."

He assured her it'd be fine; he was just grateful he wasn't stuck outside in the hallway all night. He asked her how the school nativity was going, so she spent the next twenty minutes until the pizza arrived (and she sobered up a little more) regaling him with mishaps and adorable moments and the teacher who'd tried to swan in during their second dress rehearsal today and change half the songs.

Jamie, it turned out, was a great audience. Maybe he was just being especially nice because she was letting him stay. He hadn't even made a sardonic comment about her Christmas tree yet.

And by the time they'd finished the pizzas they were barely paying attention to the movie anymore. Jamie was sat twisted towards her, one leg up on the sofa and his arm slung over the back; Eloise had her legs crossed, pizza box balanced there. He reached across to take a slice, even though he had some of his own left in the box on the floor, and she didn't even mind.

He was funny, too, now he wasn't being her grumpy neighbour.

She'd learnt more about Jamie in the past hour than she had in any conversation they'd had previously.

He worked at a mental health charity. It was a national one, with a local branch. He had a psychology degree and was a year older than her. He had three younger brothers and his family were from Nottingham, like hers. A few towns over, though. They had a couple of mutual friends on Facebook.

They had a few things in common too: a mutual love of *Star Wars*, *The Crown* and *Game of Thrones*; they'd both tried to read *Lord of the Rings* and given up after a couple of chapters; they'd both done French A levels. There were a lot of things they didn't have in common too – like the fact he thought the *Harry Potter* books weren't much cop, so hadn't read past the second one. Eloise found it hard to let that one go.

"So, right, tell me, then," she said, turning towards him and being careful not to spill her wine. They'd both had a glass, and she'd had to open another bottle. Eloise typically tried to avoid drinking on a school night, but it had been a rough day, and she figured tonight was as good as any to make an exception. She'd regret it like hell tomorrow, when she had a hangover and had to deal with another nativity practice, but right now it seemed like a great idea.

Jamie's cheeks were ruddy under his is-it-stubble-or-is-it-beard, his green eyes bright. "What?"

"Why are you always so grouchy? Like, every time we've spoken, you're just – you're like Oscar. The Grouch. Not quite a Grinch."

He laughed. It was a nice, full sound. "I'm *not* grouchy."

"You are. You're like full-on Mr Darcy."

"Please, Mr Darcy is my father."

Eloise snorted before saying, "I'm serious. Like at the start of the story. All aloof and moody."

Jamie laughed again but looked abashed. "I'm not, am I? I'm not *that* bad. I know I'm a little ... I'm a bit shy, but I'm not *aloof*."

"You so are."

"No. Nope, impossible. I've been told I'm approachable and friendly. Nobody has ever told me I'm aloof."

"Well, you are here."

"Maybe it's just because you're cute, and I'm shy."

Eloise's face was on fire in seconds, and Jamie laughed again, so at ease and smiling so widely she figured he had to be joking. He had to be, didn't he? He'd said himself, he was shy. Shy people didn't just say things like that, did they?

"I'm lucky you even opened the door to me, then, if I'm so bloody moody all the time."

"It's Christmas," Eloise said, smiling and hoping she wasn't still blushing. "'Tis the season for forgiveness and

41

goodwill and all that jazz. Even if Christmas is turning into a pile of shite this year."

"Whoa, hold on." Jamie leant towards her. "You're basically Buddy the Elf compared to most other people I know. And *you're* calling Christmas a pile of shite?"

"Well, not *Christmas* exactly," she conceded, nabbing another slice of pizza and taking a bite. She'd not even mentioned any of it to the other teachers at school, or any of her mates – because her mates were also Cara's mates, and she didn't want her sister to think she was bitching about her.

"What then?"

And despite the fact that Jamie Darcy from Number 3 was the last person she'd have imagined talking to about this, Eloise spilled it all, totally embarrassed when she even teared up a little, telling him how miserable and lonely she got sometimes, how homesick she was, how Cara didn't even seem to notice she'd abandoned her for her fabulous, flashy London lifestyle. Her wobbly voice made him look away at the TV awkwardly, not sure whether to acknowledge it or not.

"That sucks," he said eventually. "I can't imagine not spending Christmas with the family. Or going abroad for Christmas. Who wants sun, anyway? You want to go out for a walk after dinner with your breath fogging up, everyone moaning about how cold it is, and kind of wishing it'll snow but also glad it doesn't, because snow's a pain in the arse."

"Oh, my God, no! I love the snow. Everything's so pretty. Especially when it's early and nobody's been out in it yet."

Jamie pulled a face. "Nope. It's awful. Everything just comes to a standstill, and then it turns to slush and ice and that's even worse."

"Oh, humbug," she snapped, laughing. It was easier to laugh over snow than go back to talking about what a loser she was. She realised then how late it was. It had been dark since four o'clock and was raining heavily against the windows of the flat – but she realised with a start it was already past ten. She was usually fast asleep by now.

"I'll sort you out a pillow and some blankets," she said, standing and tidying some of the empty cups around, and pushing the pizza boxes out of the way. Jamie tried to help her, offered to wash up, but she waved him off. She'd sort it all tomorrow, after work. Right now, she should get to bed.

She took the couple of blankets she had off the top shelf of the wardrobe and put fresh pillowcases on two of her pillows, carrying the lot back in to Jamie. "I've got a T-shirt that should fit you, if you want something else to sleep in."

He cast a disbelieving glance over her, eyebrow arched. "Why, did you lose twelve inches? Go on a spin cycle when you're not tumble dryer-safe?"

"*Funny*. No, it's just a T-shirt I got from some night out at uni. I don't know why I've still got it, really."

She did know, but she wasn't about to share. She knew

how pathetic it'd make her sound. Eloise disappeared back to her room for the T-shirt, a black one that had a club's logo on the left side of the chest and giant white lettering on the back saying 'Don't be #whiskeysour' and '£1 shots all night'.

It wasn't even something she should have felt senti-mental about, and she knew it was stupid that she did. But Josh had been with her that night. He'd played beer pong and won the shirt, which he'd given to her. She'd worn it over her dress all night.

It was just a stupid T-shirt, but that had been the last time she'd been with Josh before everything had gone wrong.

Over five years together, and he'd ended it out of the blue to go travelling with some girl he knew from his uni course.

As if it was Eloise's fault she'd been on her teacher training and then starting a job in a primary school. As if it was *her* decision to be sensible about her career when it was just starting out that had been the last straw in their relationship. Not *his* decision to pass up a really good grad scheme and go gallivanting around Europe and Asia for months on end instead.

A holiday to Thailand – sure, she'd have loved it. But *months* backpacking around, and sacrificing a job she really wanted to do it? He'd always known that wasn't her thing.

(It hadn't been his thing either, until *Alyssa* had convinced him to go along with her.)

It didn't stop her from checking Josh's Instagram before she went to bed, though, bitterly realising how happy he was without her. He'd been updating all his social media with photos of him and his new girlfriend all over the world, rubbing salt in the wound.

It stung, when she'd worked so hard to keep their relationship together while they had been studying at different universities.

It stung even more when she thought about how she was the one who'd always had to put in that effort: he always had some excuse why he couldn't visit her, but she could come to him, or why he hadn't been able to text her back (but had no problem uploading Snapchat stories with his mates).

"'Night, Eloise," Jamie called from the living room.

She almost dropped her phone on her face, but composed herself quickly, the wine already wearing off.

"'Night."

It was nice to have someone to say goodnight to, for a change.

Chapter 5

Friday nights were the one time Cara let herself go home at five, on the dot. Like so many of the others did every other day of the week.

But this Friday it was two in the afternoon, and she and Jen had cracked open a bottle of prosecco in the loos while they did their make-up. Most of the others had gone home to get ready. Their boss, founder and CEO of Klikit, Marcus, had declared the office shut as of half eleven that morning, saying they should all go home and get ready for the Christmas party. Cara had still had a few things to finish up for the weekend, and Jen knew what she was like.

So Jen, Christmas angel that she was, and always Cara's saviour when she was in desperate need of some caffeine or a pick-me-up, had gone home, gathered her shit and brought it back into the office to get ready.

Jen knew Cara well enough that she didn't have to ask what Cara would do about her outfit. The sequinned spaghetti-strap dress was folded neatly inside her backpack, along with a clutch. She'd planned to leave her things in the office over the weekend: her keys, money and phone would fit in the clutch.

"I love you, have I mentioned that lately? You're literally the best friend ever. Like, an actual hero. The kind of hero who needs her own TV show."

"Only about three times in the last minute." Jen laughed, leaning into the mirror to fix on a fake eyelash. She grinned at Cara in the mirror. "But keep going, please. It fuels my ego."

Cara reached for the bottle of prosecco, taking a swig. Why pour it into mugs when you could just drink from the bottle? They were a classy pair: getting ready in the bathroom at work, glugging down cheap prosecco from the Tesco Express down the road at two in the afternoon, with a Spotify Christmas playlist blaring out of Jen's phone as loud as it could go.

The party wouldn't start until five-thirty, but it'd take the best part of an hour to get there in traffic.

Which gave them a solid two and a half hours to get through three bottles of prosecco (they'd been on offer, they couldn't just buy *one*) and a box of Quality Street.

Cara would've been happy to save money on a taxi and

get the Tube, but Jen had been horrified at the idea, moaning about what it would do to her hair, and had Cara *seen* the size of her heels?

"But it'll be so expensive."

"Don't be so bloody miserable. I'll pay. I'm *not* getting the Tube. I'm not putting this much effort into my make-up just to sweat it off on there."

And of course Cara wouldn't just let her pay, but she'd need a good drink before forking out that much cash on a bloody taxi. She was trying to tot up how much tonight was going to cost her before realising maybe Eloise was right. Maybe she was a bit of a Scrooge.

Cara shook it off, and took another gulp of fizz before hopping up on the counter and plucking cheap, glittery red nail varnish out of her make-up bag. No Christmas party outfit was complete without a little glitter.

There was shiny foil confetti all over the tables. White tablecloths. Silver-painted leafy centrepieces adorned with pine cones and ribbon. Piano covers of Christmas carols played gently through speakers and a photographer was hanging around in front of the giant blue-and-silver decorated Christmas tree.

Cara hiccupped. "This is goddamn adorable."

Jen giggled, squeezing her arm. "Think it's too early to start on the wine?"

"Naaah."

The bar was packed. The whole office had turned out

– all forty-three of them – and were keeping the three people behind the bar on their toes, to say the least.

"Ah, there she is!" Cara turned, and Dave was grinning at her, beer in hand. "I almost didn't expect you to show up. We thought you'd still be working."

She laughed but didn't know how to respond. Was it really such a bad thing, working hard?

"I should probably buy you a drink," he said.

"Why?"

"Hail you as my successor properly. I don't know that I'll get chance after I leave."

Cara blinked at him for a long minute. The prosecco had really gone to her head on an empty stomach. They'd only made it through a bottle and a half.

Successor.

The word took a while to register.

"Wait. Are you saying I'm – I've got it? I'm getting your job?"

Dave laughed and clapped her on the shoulder. "It's not official yet, but I've been having a word with Marcus and – let's just say it's looking good."

Cara smiled stiffly, and then Dave moved on to talk to someone else after handing her the bar's signature Christmas cocktail, a spiced red drink with a slice of artistically burnt orange peel. She manoeuvred through a few people to catch up with Jen, who was all of two feet closer to the bar, chatting to Alfie.

It's looking good wasn't exactly a guarantee. He'd really got her hopes up for a minute there.

Alfie smiled at her as she wiggled into a space near them. "Alright, C?"

"Hiya."

"Love the dress."

This time her smile was more genuine. "Thanks. Love the tie."

Alfie looked down, fingers lifting his tie a little. It was a bright red monstrosity with lurid green Christmas trees filled with tiny LEDs that flashed out of sync. "Subtlety is my strong point."

Cara had to laugh at that. Alfie was thirty-four, married with three kids, and was basically a big kid himself. He'd shown up last week in a Christmas pudding outfit. He'd grown a ridiculous walrus moustache for Movember and dyed his hair pink when they did a Race for Life in the summer.

He and Jen had cocktails to match hers, and Alfie lifted his between them. "Cheers!"

The three of them toasted. Cara wasn't sure what was in the drink; it tasted strong, and she took another sip. It was *good*.

"So, have they told you yet? Are you going to be the new boss?"

Jen slung an arm around her. "Of course she is! This is Cara we're talking about. She's a *machine*."

"I've not heard anything for definite," she said. Sure, Dave had sounded confident, and he wouldn't have said anything if he didn't think she'd get it, but she was scared of jinxing it. She poked her orange peel around with the straw. "And I wouldn't be the boss."

"Might as well be. You'll be running this place in two years. Mark my words."

"Don't let Marcus hear you saying that," Jen mock-scolded, then giggled. "We need him in a good mood if he's going to buy everyone a round later."

Conversation turned to plans for Christmas. Alfie and his husband were taking the kids to visit their grandparents in Devon. Jen was going home to her family in Brighton. Bryan, from the digital team, had joined them, and mentioned he was heading up to Scotland for Hogmanay with his family.

"What about you?" they asked when Cara didn't contribute.

"Oh. I'm not sure."

They stared at her.

"Well, I did have a bus booked to go home, but I'm not sure I'll go. I can get it refunded," she explained, but they just kept staring at her like she'd gone mad. It made her stomach twist, though, because she really should've talked to Eloise about this properly. What was she going to do? She was supposed to be in work by the twenty-seventh. Would Eloise visit her? And if she did come to visit, would she expect Cara to cook a whole turkey, all the trimmings?

Would she be fine with some bacon sarnies and Bucks Fizz?

Cara had another drink. If people kept asking her about this, it was going to be a *really* long night.

"Oh, thank God." Jen let her go and stood up. "Seriously. Thank you so much. I really appreciate this. I can't tell you how much I love you right now."

Someone laughed. A guy. It was a nice laugh. Like a laugh she knew. Cara's head drifted upwards and her lips curved into a smile, eyes drooping as she leant against the lamppost. "*George*. Hello." The words were long. Her tongue was heavy. She smiled wider.

"Oh, Jesus," he said, and laughed again. Cara peeled her eyes open long enough to see Jen handing over a clutch that looked just like hers (and, oh, fuck, where was her clutch? She'd lost it, and her phone, her keys, her – no, that *was* her clutch).

The two of them hoisted Cara to her feet, where she swayed before throwing her arms around Jen, planting a sloppy kiss on her cheek. "I love you. You're the best. You're my favourite best friend. Did you know that? Of all my best friends, you're my favourite."

Jen extracted herself and Cara flopped into George's arms instead, turning and twisting her head up to give him a kiss. He had lovely lips.

Lovely lips that she missed because he moved, and she kissed somewhere on his jaw instead. Not that she minded. He had a lovely jaw too. He was very lovely.

"You're very lovely."

George laughed again. She didn't know why it was so funny; he *was* lovely.

He'd turned his head away from her kiss, though, and he replied, "I'm going to get drunk just off those fumes. How much did you drink?"

"Seven."

"Seven what?"

"*Se-ven!*" she shouted, imitating Len Goodman from *Strictly*, and bursting into a fit of giggles. "I like this song. Can we dance? Let's rock around the Christmas tree. You can be the tree."

Jen huffed behind her. "If you can't handle this, tell me now, before I go back into the party."

"I can handle this."

Jen hugged her with one arm and then gave her a very serious look, all big eyes and pinched mouth. She turned the look on George. "You be careful with her. And text me as soon as you get her home. I want proof she's okay. My number's in her phone. Pin's five-six-eight-three."

"Five-six-eight-three. Got it."

Jen squeezed her hand and then she was gone, going back inside the bar.

George's arm went around her waist, and Cara leaned her head on his shoulder. He smelled lovely too.

The taxi didn't.

She fumbled in the taxi, looking at George with panicked

eyes. She could feel them bulging out of their sockets. "My bag. I forgot my bag. I've lost my bag."

"I've got your bag." He held it up, smiling, and she sagged against the seat.

"Is my phone in there?"

He checked. "One phone, one wallet, one set of keys, one lipstick, one strip of raffle tickets and – why did you bring an Amazon voucher with you to your Christmas party?"

She leaned over, almost fell into his lap, and looked into the bag. "Oh! I won it! In the raffle!"

"Just as well you didn't win a bottle of wine." He laughed. To the taxi driver: "Left up here, please, mate. Yeah – it's about halfway down. Blue door."

When the taxi stopped, she tried to take her bag back from George to get some money out, but he brushed her away gently and paid and helped her out of the taxi. He walked her up to a door as the taxi drove off.

It was like her door.

He put her keys in and she realised it *was* her door.

She tripped inside, George only just catching her arm to keep her upright, and she laughed, pressed a finger to her lips, shouted, "Shhh!" and staggered in the direction of the staircase. She tipped forwards, body moving before her legs did, hands planting on the stairs. That was okay. She could crawl up. That would be fun.

George stood her back up.

The stairs went on *forever*.

She collapsed on the bed, limbs splayed out like she was making a snow angel. She waggled her feet. "Can you help take my shoes off? Oh, no, don't! Never mind! No, don't take my shoes off. My feet smell."

George pulled one shoe off and made a big show of collapsing from the stink of it.

"It's fine," he told her, reaching for the other shoe. She stuck her leg towards him. "I'm part ogre. I'm used to this kind of stench."

"Thanks, Shrek," she said, meaning it, legs falling back onto the bed. Her feet hung off the end. Her head wasn't quite on the pillow. She watched George use her phone. "How do you know my passcode?"

"Jen told me. She wanted to know you were home safe." She heard the camera shutter click. "Just sending proof I haven't kidnapped you or left you in a ditch somewhere."

"Thank you for not leaving me in a ditch."

He sat beside her on the bed. "You're going to really hate yourself in the morning."

"I think I hate myself a bit right now," she confessed.

"Right. I can fix this. What you need is water and coffee and pizza. Think you can stay awake that long?"

"No."

"Think you can stay awake long enough for me to get you water from the kitchen, at least?"

"No." But she had some bottles of water on the bottom shelf of her little bookcase. She lurched sideways on the bed, arm out like she could reach the four feet to the water bottles without moving any further.

George put one in her hand.

"You're the best. I love you."

"Do you now?" When she looked at him, he was smiling, lips pressed together like he was trying not to. His eyes were sparkly, like her dress.

"Yes." She leant up far enough to drink some of the water, handed it back to him and fell back onto the bed again. Mm, bed. Bliss.

She'd barely closed her eyes when she groaned. "I really fucked up." Embarrassment was one thing. Reliving it all over again was another. "I bet I've lost the promotion now. Getting absolutely rat-arsed. Oh, shit."

"I'm sure you didn't. Everyone goes a bit mad at their Christmas party. They have to. It's Christmas. They'll all have a laugh about the state you got into on Monday and then they'll forget until next year."

Cara groaned again, rolling towards him, hands covering her face. Her dress crinkled, the sequins stiff and protesting. "I need to put my pyjamas on," she told him. "Turn around."

She was a bit surprised when he did, and she managed to stand long enough to shimmy out of the dress and pull on the oversized T-shirt from some society she'd joined at uni that she used as pyjamas.

"Thank you for coming to get me."

"That's alright. You know you kept ringing me? When

57

you were in the bar. Telling me you loved me and wanted me to come to meet all your friends. You sang *Fairytale of New York* to me."

"I did?"

"Both parts. It was atrocious."

"Fuck you."

"Two minutes ago you loved me."

"Yes, well, then you insulted my singing." Cara buried herself under the covers and peeked out from under them. George was looking at her with one side of his mouth twisted up and his head cocked. "What?"

"In the least creepy way possible, is it okay if I stay? I'm kind of worried you're going to vomit. You look a bit dodgy. Where's your bin?" He got up to look for it, moving it next to the bed.

"*You're* dodgy," she muttered back.

"I'm taking that as a no, then."

"My wit is lost on you," she lamented, rolling onto her back. She yanked one half of the covers back. "You can stay. I'm not going to be sick, but you can stay. And if I'm sick on you, it's not my fault."

When she woke up six hours later, George was snoring next to her, her tongue was too big for her mouth, her head was pounding and she had never felt more embarrassed in her entire life. She didn't even dare reach for her phone to see what kind of awful, humiliating things she might have taken photos of or messages she might have sent last night.

Cara closed her eyes again. Hopefully, she'd sleep through the next few hours and sleep off this hangover.

Although at that point, she wouldn't mind sleeping right through Christmas and the New Year too.

Chapter 6

"Ughhhhhhhh," Cara groaned down the phone to her.

Eloise bit back a laugh and tried to sound sympathetic when she replied, "Fun night?"

"The complete opposite."

Eloise touched the brush of the nail varnish against the pot to get rid of the excess before gliding it over the nail of her index finger. It was only a cheap nail polish, but red and glittery. It'd be good enough to last through the night for her party. "What happened?"

Cara just groaned again.

"It can't have been that bad."

"Believe me, it was. We'd been drinking since two and I just kept going. Mixed my drinks. Had loads of these

61

really fun cocktails but no idea what was in them. Then we all did jagerbombs at the bar we went to afterwards."

"Tell me you at least stayed away from the tequila."

Her sister's silence was answer enough.

"Oh, Cara, you *know* you can't handle tequila."

"Someone bought a whole round of them. I was such a mess. I made a complete idiot of myself. Jen said I told Marcus I'd be running the place in two years."

Eloise gasped before she could stop herself, hand flying to her mouth. "Oh my God. You didn't."

"Apparently, I did. Apparently, they all thought it was hilarious. I'm blaming Alfie. He said it first, put it in my head. I was home by midnight."

"Bloody hell, Cinderella. How did you even manage to get home in that state? You didn't take the Tube, did you? You could've got on the wrong line. Fallen off the platform –"

"Yes, alright, *Mum*. I got a taxi. Jen had to get George to come and pick me up."

"What, and he actually came?"

"He did."

"He's a saint."

"I kept telling him I loved him."

Eloise did let out a giggle at that. Cara was a really affectionate drunk. Always chatty, taking selfies with everyone, buying drinks for everyone, hugging everyone. Her smile faded a little; imagining it made her miss her sister.

"He was kind of weird this morning, though," Cara mused, and Eloise frowned at the phone, a blob of nail varnish falling onto her hand.

"Shit," she muttered. Then, "He stayed the night? Oh my God, you didn't have sex with him, did you? Not when you were that drunk?"

"No! Of course we didn't. He stayed to make sure I didn't puke in my sleep. That's not the point, anyway. He was on the phone to someone this morning. He was talking really quiet, so I didn't catch most of it. He thought I was still asleep. I don't know, he just sounded ... like, affectionate. Close, you know? He said something about someone called Lina, and that he'd be over soon, and then when I *woke up* –" Eloise could picture Cara's face screwed up sideways and the air quotes "– he said he had to get off home. He just kind of rushed off, which is weird, right?"

"Um –"

"Because if she was just a mate he'd have said he was going to meet a mate, and he's literally never mentioned anyone called Lina or anything remotely similar to me before, and he was really sweet coming to get me last night and looking after me when I was smashed and then he just ran off. Didn't even stay for a cuppa."

"Didn't even make you a cuppa, you mean."

"That too. But it's weird, right? That's weird. I'm not overreacting?"

"You could've just asked him." Not that Eloise would've

asked if she'd been in Cara's situation. She'd be doing exactly the same thing – overreacting, phoning her sister and asking if it was weird and if she was being crazy.

"He's twenty-four, right?"

"Yeah. So?"

"Maybe he's got kids."

"I feel like he'd have mentioned that."

"Jude Law doesn't in *The Holiday*."

Cara groaned. "That's it. You're officially useless."

"I'm just saying! Maybe there's a totally innocent explanation. Best thing to do is just ask him outright. And then, if you're still suspicious, then ... I don't know. Check his messages? Is that too drastic?"

She hadn't done any of that with Josh. She'd thought she was overreacting and being paranoid and she just had to work a little harder at their relationship. She'd got too comfortable and she'd stopped trying, or something. She had to make more of an effort. It was all on her, she'd thought, and she would trust him. She had to, if she wanted things to work.

Maybe she should've checked his messages. Maybe then it wouldn't have been such a shock to hear he was going travelling with another girl.

"I don't know." Cara's voice was dry and scathing. "What would Jude Law do?"

"You're so mean when you're hungover."

"I'm mean when my job is potentially on the line. And I might have jeopardised my chance at a promotion."

"Don't be so dramatic. It was the Christmas party. Shit happens."

"Not to *me*."

Of course it didn't. Shit never happened to perfect, proper Cara.

"If it's that bad, take a few days off. Go back to Mum and Dad's, let it all die down. Or work from home or something, say you're not feeling well."

"I'm not running back home," Cara snapped. "I can handle my own problems."

The *unlike you* was left hanging in the air. Eloise had gone back home and hardly left her bed for a week after the break-up with Josh. Cara had dragged her back to uni for the last few weeks until graduation when she wanted nothing more than to wallow and delete all their pictures off her Instagram. Cara never let her forget it, acting like she was such a child for wanting to go home to get some sympathy and support. Like she was so much *better*.

Eloise scowled for a moment before concentrating back on the next coat of nail varnish. "What do you want me to say, Cara?"

Nothing, apparently. Her sister didn't respond. Eloise was willing to bet she was pouting, mouthing and mimicking her silently.

Eventually, Eloise sighed. "Order some food. Drink some tea. I'll talk to you tomorrow. We need to talk about Christmas."

"Enjoy your party."

"Thanks." Eloise noticed Cara didn't comment on how they needed to talk about Christmas. Every time she'd tried to bring it up lately, Cara suddenly had to rush off, do something else, stop talking. Eloise was trying so hard not to let on how desperate she felt about it. She didn't think she could face the holiday alone.

It'd probably be Boxing Day before Cara wanted to talk about what they were doing for Christmas.

Eloise had just collected her post from the letterbox by the main entrance to the building when Jamie pulled up in his car. She held the door open, and he waved as he gathered bulging carrier bags from his boot.

"Don't tell me you're only buying gifts the week before Christmas," she commented, nodding at them.

"When else would I buy them?"

"I start in October. September, sometimes, if I see something I want to get someone."

He shook his head, smiling a little. They hadn't talked much since he'd spent the night on her sofa, and she was almost disappointed about that. Not sure why, exactly, but she was.

"Going somewhere nice?" he asked, taking in the sparkly nail varnish, the make-up – and the rollers in her hair were kind of hard to miss. "Hot date?"

Eloise patted the rollers and laughed and – oh, God, she wasn't blushing, was she? Her cheeks felt like they were on fire. Could he tell?

When – *WHEN* – had she even developed this stupid crush on him? When had that even happened? Before or after he'd spent the night? Had he always been this cute – because, seriously, how had she never noticed how attractive he was? With that smile and that *jaw* and those eyes?

It had to be the glasses. She'd never fancied him before she'd seen him in glasses.

Although he wasn't wearing them now, and her stomach still felt fluttery.

"It's my work Christmas do," she explained. "Last week before school lets out, you know. It's nothing fancy. We've got a table booked at the Red Lion pub."

"Oh. Maybe I'll see you there later." When she cocked her head at him questioningly, Jamie added, "I'm meeting a couple of mates there later."

"Well." They were both at their doors now, standing across the hallway from each other. Eloise clutched her post to her chest. "See you later, I guess."

Her cheeks ached from laughing so hard. Eloise slumped over the bar, trying to get someone's attention. Nobody had been round at their table for ages, so she'd volunteered to ask for more drinks.

And she'd totally *not* volunteered in the hope of catching sight of Jamie. Absolutely not. She wasn't that desperate.

But she did grin when a hand settled between her shoulder blades and she turned to see him there. "Hey!"

"Hey yourself."

His lips stretched out in a slow smile, eyes fixed on hers, and Eloise felt her insides melt. Oh, God, she was so pathetic. Swooning over his brown hair that he'd styled into a quiff for the night and the fact he was in a shirt with the top couple of buttons open and he'd shaved and –

She was so, so far past pathetic.

"Having a good night?" she asked, hoping he hadn't noticed her staring.

"Yeah, not too bad! Apparently, I missed the Christmas jumper memo, though, so I've been buying most of the drinks all night."

"Rookie."

"I don't see you wearing one."

Was it just a glass too much wine, or did his eyes linger when they took in her sparkly black and silver dress and matching bright silver heeled pumps?

"I took it off. It's too warm in here."

He smiled again, biting his lower lip a little. Oh, God, did he have to do that? Now she was staring at his lips. It seemed to take an inordinate amount of effort for Eloise to drag her eyes back up to his. "You wore a Christmas jumper over your dress?"

"Duh."

"And –" Jamie's hand reached out, pushing her curls back over her shoulder; Eloise shuddered when his fingers brushed her neck and he lifted her earring. Giant wreaths, tacky as hell, with little jingle bells. "Bloody hell. They're big enough to hang off a tree. Are you sure they're not meant to be ornaments?"

She laughed, and he let go of the earring. His hand was slow to move away from her neck. Or maybe she was just imagining it.

A barman finally made his way over and Eloise turned her attention back, asking if they could send some drinks over to their table, reeling off the list she'd made a note of on her phone.

"And here was me thinking I could buy you a drink," Jamie said. She jumped, not realising how close he was, and her body knocked against his. "And I know it's Christmas and all, but I am *not* picking up that tab."

Eloise laughed again, feeling another blush rise. God. She hadn't been this giddy around a guy in – in *ever*. She hadn't even been like this with Josh. With Josh, it had been months of occasional awkward dates, stiff and trying-to-flirt texts, and then suddenly they were in a relationship.

And she definitely hadn't been this giddy around any of the random Tinder dates she'd been on recently.

"You were going to buy me a drink?"

Jamie smiled at her. "Guess you'll never know, now."

"Well ..." She glanced back towards the part of the pub where her Christmas party was. "These guys have all got taxis or lifts home in about half an hour. If you're still around then, you can buy me a drink."

"Oh, I can, can I?" Someone pushed past behind him,

jostling them closer together. A thrill fizzed through Eloise. She had to get a grip. She was turning into an actual loser.

"Since you asked so nicely."

"Bet I can guess your poison."

"Yeah?"

"Tap water. Slice of lemon, if you're feeling extravagant."

She laughed. "Watch it, big spender. You can't just make a big offer like that. For all you know, I could be looking for some rich sap to marry and fund my Christmas earring collection."

"I mean," he chuckled, reaching for the earring again, disappointing her when his fingers didn't touch her skin again, "they look *crazy* expensive. He'll need to be a very rich sap."

Eloise smiled back. She was too busy enjoying the smell of his aftershave to come up with a flirty reply. "Well, I'd, um, better get back. Last lot of drinks before everyone starts heading home." Most of the teachers had families, and they'd been out for the best part of four hours, now. Jamie kept smiling at her, and stepped half out of the way, so she brushed up against him as she scooted past.

She glanced back at him, and he was still looking at her. Still smiling that little smile, eyes twinkling.

Not that she minded. At all.

Her whole body felt like a shaken-up bottle of champagne.

Seriously, *when* had this happened? When had she developed such a raging crush on Jamie Darcy, of all people?

She loitered at the table until the last few teachers were pulling on their coats to go home. A couple had stayed sober to drive, but the table was covered in empty wine and beer bottles nonetheless.

Eloise gathered her coat, scarf, Christmas jumper and bag and made her way back to the bar. She didn't expect Jamie to still be there – her party had ended up going on for another hour before people were really setting off – but she wanted him to be.

She wasn't disappointed.

He was sitting at the bar on his phone, nursing a nearly empty pint.

She should duck out. Beg a lift off someone. Go wait outside and call for a taxi. He hadn't noticed her yet and she could just go.

She hadn't felt this way about anyone in – well, ever. And that scared her. And maybe he didn't even really like her that much. Maybe she was just here, and he wanted something casual and fun.

Which might be fine, but – if the way her heart was racing was anything to go by – she already liked him a little too much to want some fling and nothing more.

She could just go. Should just go.

Her hand reached out for the bar, feet already moving,

as she pulled herself onto the tall chair beside him. "What happened to all your mates?"

"They went home."

She stared at him. "Did you wait for me?"

"Maybe." He blushed but grinned at her.

He was definitely flirting. Definitely interested. The only question was *how* interested?

"So, what're you drinking?"

"Surprise me."

They only had the one drink – gin and lemonade for Eloise, a cider for Jamie – but stayed in the pub until closing, chatting easily and flirting openly. And the flirting went well, for the most part, as far as she could tell. The only exception was when he made Eloise laugh so hard she snorted into her drink and choked on it.

But their bodies were tilted towards each other, knees knocking, and his hand was on her thigh. It was warm. Maybe a little sweaty, but she didn't mind. She was a little sweaty too.

When they were turned out for closing, Eloise was a little tipsy. Not enough to be oblivious to the cold, though. Jamie called a taxi firm, telling her it'd be ten minutes until they got picked up. Ten minutes too long, she thought. Her teeth chattered, and she shoved her coat towards Jamie to pull on her Christmas jumper. It was halfway on when he grabbed her hips, the warmth of his body almost touching hers.

"Should I take it as a bad sign you're putting more clothes on?"

"Don't be a prick," she said, wiggling her arms through the jumper. She felt her curls spring out around her once her head was through, static. She took her coat back, pulling it on and zipping it right up.

Jamie was laughing, though, and she realised he wasn't being serious. She kind of wanted him to be.

"You're going to have to at least kiss me first," she said. "Unluckily for you, I don't have any mistletoe."

Jamie took his phone out. End of conversation apparently.

She shouldn't be so surprised. Maybe she should've just kissed him instead.

Then he turned it towards her, holding it up. A picture of mistletoe took up the screen. Eloise giggled. "That'll do."

Eloise tilted her head up, meeting him halfway. Her whole body turned to goo at the press of his soft lips against hers, the way his hands held her waist and seemed to make her skin burn even though she had three layers in the way.

He drew away too quickly, leaving Eloise perched on her toes, eyes closed, lips puckered out, feeling like she might just float away.

A horn beeped.

Their ride home was here.

Ten days till Christmas

Chapter 7

Cara read the text in utter disbelief.

> *Okay, YES, we had sex, and YES, it was aaaaamazing,*
> *but it's so not going anywhere*

No way. She'd asked the question after Eloise had sent her essays about her unexpected date night after the Christmas work party (which had been much more sober and less humiliating than Cara's, and Eloise had been good enough not to rub that in) – but Cara had never actually expected that response.

> *YOU DID NOT. OH MY GOD. Not with Mr Arsey*
> *himself?!*

... and is that because YOU don't want it to go anywhere or he doesn't?

Um. Next question please

You should just ask him, you know

I'll ask him when you ask George about Lina

Cara shot back a few emojis, unimpressed, and Eloise stopped replying.

They still hadn't talked about Christmas. She was putting that off as long as she could. Eloise should just grow up already. Just because it was the holidays didn't mean they didn't have responsibilities any more, or shit to do. Not everyone got a couple of weeks off work at this time of year.

Plus, Eloise could have that insufferable attitude sometimes of acting like Cara needed her help. She could cope just fine on her own, thank you very much.

Although she still hadn't figured out what to do about George.

They'd text and when she'd asked what he was doing he just said he was watching TV. Not even 'with a friend'. He didn't say he was out somewhere. Did that mean Lina, whoever she was, had met him at his place?

She couldn't just *ask* him. It'd be weird if she asked him now after pretending to be asleep when he took the phone call and not bringing it up yesterday morning. And she'd sound crazy if she asked if he was with someone, seemingly out of the blue.

It wasn't like she'd spent the *whole* weekend agonising over it … not like she'd spent the weekend agonising over how atrociously she'd behaved at the Christmas do on Friday night.

George was the easier of the two to worry about and overthink. She liked him, a lot – but if she lost him now, so what? Alright, maybe she'd be a little heartbroken, and she'd miss him, and her mum would be disappointed when she'd said so many good things about him. But so what? He was a guy. There were other guys out there.

Her job, though. That was something she couldn't afford to lose.

Desperate not to sink into the dark spiral of her hideous weekend, Cara hauled herself off the bed. It was past ten. She'd spent her entire Saturday moping; time to get her shit together.

By midday, she'd done her share of the household chores and cleaned her room, done some laundry, and washed and dried her hair. She'd phoned her parents to chat, and made out like she hadn't been utterly smashed at the party, milling around the kitchen as she talked.

"Have you and Eloise decided what you're doing for Christmas yet? Will you be coming home, or doing it at one of yours? It'd make sense for you to go to Eloise's, you know; it'll be easier to do the cooking without worrying about anybody else in your house. You can just have a nice little one then, and you won't need to do a full turkey. Or are you skipping the roast altogether? Shall I look up some other Christmassy recipes for you? I'll send you some links on Pinterest. Eloise knows how busy you are with work; I'm sure she can knock something together for you both."

"That's okay, Mum. I'm sure we can sort something between us," Cara protested, knowing her mum would send her twenty 'unique' twists on Christmas dinner alternatives within the next hour. "And we've not decided yet."

"Well, you'll need to get a move on. The trains will be getting expensive, and they'll all be booked up. Ooh, maybe you should ask that George to spend Christmas with you, if he's alone as well. That might be nice."

"Yes, maybe ... He might have plans, though. I'll see. I've got to go now, Mum. I'll call you in the week."

"Alright, darling, bye-bye."

Christmas with George? Two days ago she'd have been daydreaming about it. Now, not so much.

Cara threw open her bedroom windows, having almost gagged at the lingering stench of hangover in her room when she got back to it. She'd regret it later when her room was frozen solid, but at least it wouldn't smell. She'd just throw some extra blankets on the bed.

Afraid that if she stayed in her room she'd undo her

not-exactly-good-but-at-least-improved mood, Cara decided to go out – out into the Christmas chaos.

The house was half-empty, but she knocked on the rooms of her housemates to see if anybody wanted to go out to Oxford Street or maybe Camden, or Covent Garden. In the end, she left the house on her own.

Cara milled around Oxford Street for an hour, weaving around counters in Selfridges and dipping in and out of shops. She didn't buy anything, though.

Why would she? She'd already sorted everyone's presents. She'd had some Euros delivered to her parents, as well as the usual suspects of Baileys and a scarf and mitten set from Next for her mum, and the Marks & Spencer's port her dad liked with some Amazon vouchers. She knew Eloise would've put it all together in a nice hamper along with her gifts for their parents, with a few little extras, and she'd have wrapped it beautifully.

Cara had just clenched her teeth and paid the extra cost online for gift wrap. It was such a waste. It wasn't like they'd see the bottle-shaped packages and think, *Oh, look, Cara got us books this year!*

She had Eloise's presents back at the flat. A Christmas Pandora charm for the bracelet she wore, some Hotel Chocolat, and a Bumble and bumble product she used religiously. It was a small pile, but all things she knew her sister would love, and none of it was exactly bargain basement.

Without any shopping to do, though, and not wanting

to buy anything for herself this close to Christmas, Oxford Street was just awful after an hour. The lights were on and the sky was dark and gloomy with clouds, but it didn't feel cute and Christmassy.

It was just loud. People kept banging into her, laden down with bags. Christmas songs blared out of open shop fronts, clashing with each other into one cacophony of jingle bells.

She couldn't stay out shopping.

This was unbearable.

But she couldn't go home, either.

And she couldn't see if George was free. He'd not replied to her texts in hours. Not even liked the Facebook post she'd tagged him in a little while ago, even though she could see he'd been active.

Not that she was checking. But she'd noticed.

What if he was with Lina?

That spiral again. Not as bad as her worries about her job, but still bad enough to make her feel shitty about herself.

And God, she was calling him. Why was she doing that? Why was she even –

"Hello, Cara." He sounded so normal. Pleased to hear from her. She knew him well enough that it sounded like he was smiling.

"Um, hi. I was just ... I'm just around the shops. I wondered if you're around? Maybe get some food? Or I could come to yours for a bit, if you're free?"

In one of the few texts she'd had from him today, when she'd asked that morning what his plans for the day were, he'd said –

Absolutely nothing. You?

But he sighed, heavily. Said, "Oh, no, I'm sorry, darling." She had liked that he called her darling. It seemed kind of old-fashioned. It seemed cuter than babe. Now, it grated on her. Sounded pretentious. "I'm a bit busy right now. I've, um, I'm ... working. We've got some accounts signing this week, and the deadline's bumped up a few days. All hands on deck. It's really not a good time right now."

Liar. He was a terrible liar. She was so tempted to call him out on it.

"Oh. Right, yeah, sure. No problem."

"I'm sorry. Maybe later this week?"

Was it just her imagination, or did that sound like the world's biggest brush-off? The kind of, 'Oh, yes, we must get drinks and catch up soon!' you didn't really mean but felt obliged to offer up.

Cara hedged her bets. "I might be a bit busy with work." If she even still had a job ... "You know what it's like. All hands on deck."

George was quiet for a moment. "Well, let me know. I'll text you later. Enjoy shopping."

He hung up quickly, but not before she thought she heard another voice in the background. Rationality told her it was music, a housemate, a TV show. But her heart was hammering right out of her ribcage and seemed to be screaming at her, *Don't believe a goddamn word of it, Cara, he's with her, with that Lina, whoever she is.*

Maybe he was.

Had they ever even actually said they were exclusive? She was sure they'd had that conversation, but maybe they hadn't. Maybe she'd just assumed and inferred.

Maybe she'd just let herself start to fall for him and was a prize fool.

She snorted at herself, drawing the attention of two people standing nearby. *Start to fall for him.* Yeah, right. She'd known he was the sort of guy she could fall in love with right from the off, and their first couple of dates had only proved that. The last few weeks, when they'd seen more of each other, she knew it was already too late. Too quickly, probably, but still too late. He was everything she could have dreamt of.

Except for the part where she felt pretty certain he'd been lying to her all weekend.

The worst part was that it didn't even make any sense. He'd been her knight in shining armour at the party. He'd talked again earlier in the week about her meeting his parents in the New Year. You didn't do that with someone you were cheating on, did you? Or someone you didn't want to be with?

Then again – what would she know?

Cara's longest relationship had been six months, with a

boy in sixth form. She'd been on a couple of dates with someone in first year and been with a guy from her course for four or five months in second year, but the whole romance thing just hadn't happened for her. Not like it had for Eloise, with Josh. Not like it had for her now, with George.

It wasn't like she'd *sacrificed* relationships and romance to get through her degree and then for her job – she'd been more than open to it. It just hadn't happened. Which was fine and had never bothered her before. But it did mean she was lacking in experience when it came to relationship problems.

Like what to do when you think your boyfriend is lying to you.

(Google wasn't very helpful, when she asked it.)

Cara found herself in a bookstore. There was a three-for-two promotion stand near the front with Christmas books. The classic Charles Dickens, the year's newest cookbooks for the holidays, some kids' books, and a shelf of bright coloured covers with swirly title fonts that screamed romance.

Romance should've been the last thing on her mind this weekend, but her hands were already reaching out, plucking books down to read the blurbs.

Maybe a little romance was *exactly* what she needed right now, she realised.

George wasn't a bad guy. What kind of guy would have

come to take her home from her Christmas party, stayed up to make sure she was alright? A good guy, she answered herself. Like George.

Just because Eloise's boyfriend had shocked them all by running off around Europe with some random girl from university when they'd all expected him to propose didn't mean George was a lying, cheating scumbag too.

She was willing to give him the benefit of the doubt. Wanted to.

Perhaps it was the quiet of the bookshop, or the optimistic and slightly cheesy descriptions on the backs of the romance books, or the fact she hadn't read anything longer than a few thousand words of an article online at a time in the last two years, but Cara knew exactly how she wanted to spend her afternoon. She grabbed three of the books at random and headed for the tills, grinning at the thought of spending the next couple of hours holed up in a coffee shop out of the way somewhere with one of them, and curling up in bed to finish it later.

Ten days till Christmas

Chapter 8

Eloise bent her head forward, letting the hot water pound the back of her neck for a long moment before reaching for the shampoo. She screwed up her face for a moment as she lathered her hair up.

Bloody hell. What had she done? Having sex with him last night? Was she absolutely bonkers? Cara seemed to think so. Eloise played the night back over in her head, running through it as if she could pinpoint exactly when she'd lost the plot.

Instead she just started smiling, feeling warm inside in a way that had nothing to do with the shower, until she realised she was bordering on goofy and bit her lip to try and get rid of the smile.

What she hadn't mentioned to Cara was that she'd snuck out before he'd woken up.

Her goofy smile turned into a grimace. She groaned, covering her face with her hands.

They'd gone back to his flat last night, and Eloise had been shocked to see a small Christmas tree, but then they'd been too busy snogging and tearing each other's clothes off and laughing when her Christmas jumper got stuck around her head and tangled in her earrings. And then this morning she'd woken up first and waited for a few minutes before grabbing her stuff, pulling on her coat and making a not-quite-nude dash across the hall to her own flat.

Where she'd text her sister and then taken a shower.

She'd been too freaked out at the idea of him waking up and the whole 'What next?' question that had been scrambling her brain to stick around.

This wasn't like her. She didn't just sleep with guys.

Well, alright, not like *this*. There may have been one or two one-night stands since Josh, but those were different. Those were guys she barely knew and was happy to keep it that way.

But she *liked* Jamie.

As was evidenced by the lovestruck feeling she had around him lately.

She felt too stupid to message any of her friends for advice. Because how the hell did that sound? *I think I really like this guy and we slept together and I ran out on him before he woke up.*

It made her sound like a right cotton-headed ninny-muggins, that's what.

Eloise was barely out of the shower, hair and body wrapped in towels, when there was a knock on her door.

Three guesses who, she thought, and shoved her feet into her slippers before crossing from her bathroom to the door. She'd put the chain on, out of habit, and opened it like that – all of two inches. Enough to peer out through the gap.

Oh, God, how did he look so much better all sleepy and dishevelled? He was in the boxers he'd been wearing last night and a hoodie, hands buried in the pockets of it, brown hair stuck up and out at odd angles. It looked so soft she just wanted to run her fingers through it. And he had his glasses on. She'd forgotten how well they suited him – and how much hotter they made him look.

He arched an eyebrow, expression guarded. "Um, wow. I'm taking it as a really bad sign you won't even open your door to me properly. If I upset you, or did something ..."

"You didn't," she admitted, and closed the door. Undid the chain and opened it again. Eloise opened it wide, but stayed half behind it, clutching her towel tight to her. She noticed his eyes dip a little, but then focus back on her face.

"Are you sure? Because you left at some point, without telling me, and now you can't even look at me."

He didn't sound pissed off, just confused. Kind of hurt. A bit concerned. Eloise's eyes flicked back up to his, which was when she realised he was right. She'd been avoiding looking at him properly.

Not for the reasons he thought.

Only because he was so damn cute it made her heart thud in weird patterns.

"Yes, I'm sure. It wasn't anything you did. I just ... thought I should come back home."

Jamie studied her face for forever. The moment seemed to stretch and she shifted her weight to the other foot, not sure how to explain herself. He looked down, then rocked back and forth once on his heels.

"So, this was just a one-time thing." He said it like a fact. Looked her in the eyes.

"Um. I mean, I ... I guess?" How the hell did people handle this? Everything she'd read online and everything her friends told her was lies. Casual sex made everything so much more complicated. "If you want."

"What do you want?"

"Loaded question. What are we talking, here? In life? In the next five years? Right now?"

He didn't laugh, like she hoped he would, because at least if he was laughing everything was okay and she could pretend that she hadn't screwed up whatever this might have been.

A door opened on the floor above. Alarm flit over Jamie's face briefly. "Do you mind if we carry on this conversation inside?"

The footsteps of someone leaving Number Six sounded

on the stairs, and Eloise nodded and let him come in, dreading the thought of a neighbour (well, *another* neighbour) seeing her in her towel more than she did the idea of having this awkward conversation.

That thought came after she shut the door.

"Can you give me two seconds? I'll just put some clothes on."

He nodded. "I could make a cup of tea?"

"Er, okay, yes, please." What else was she supposed to say? Besides – a cuppa definitely wouldn't go amiss. She hadn't had one since she'd woken up.

Tea could fix anything. With any luck, it'd fix this situation too.

Eloise dressed frantically, pulling on the leggings from her chair and grabbing a clean T-shirt before remembering she should probably put on a bra, and then realised she'd left her bra from yesterday at Jamie's.

She'd have to get that back. It was her best one. And bloody expensive.

She met him back in the kitchen, her hair soaking through the back of her cardigan and T-shirt, and no make-up on. At least no make-up was a better look than smudged foundation and panda eyes.

He passed her a mug. "I don't really know how this is supposed to work," he said.

"How what is?"

"This. Hooking up. One-night stands."

"Oh. Me either, really. At least, not like this." Then she

blurted, "I've only been in one serious relationship, and more or less every date I've been on since then has been a total disaster."

"Ouch. Total disaster. Really?"

"You're classing last night as a date?"

"Maybe a little." He flashed her a cheeky smile and Eloise felt herself relaxing. How was that smile better at relaxing her than a hot shower had been? Then, more serious, the smile dropping away, Jamie cupped his hands tighter around his mug and asked her, "Why did you run out this morning, then?"

Because I think I really like you and I didn't want to get hurt.

"I just really, really had to fart."

Jamie burst into laughter, eyes creasing, mouth wide, and she laughed too.

At least he got her sense of humour.

"I'm sorry. Was it a shitty thing to do? I just sort of panicked. Which is not a comment on the night – or date, I guess – *at all*. I just didn't really know what to do. I thought there'd be an awkward conversation when we were both awake and ..."

"And you think me knocking on your door in my pants isn't an awkward conversation?"

"Alright, point taken." Eloise turned to lean against the counter, facing him sideways now, and sipped her tea. "Hypothetically, then. If I hadn't done a disappearing act this morning. How would that have gone?"

"Well." Jamie set down his mug, stepping closer. It only

took two strides for him to be in front of her. Carefully, he took the mug from her hands, reaching around to put it on the counter too. Every action seemed to be agonisingly slow. Eloise realised she was holding her breath and let it out, acutely aware of how loud and heavy and shallow it sounded.

Jamie cupped her cheek. "It might have started like this."

He kissed her. Slowly, softly. His glasses butted against her face a little. His lips were light on hers, and when he drew back, they ghosted over her cheek. "Hypothetically."

Eloise felt heat rise in her cheeks. She was *this close* to yanking him towards the bedroom. Right now it was hard to remember why that was such a bad idea.

"Kind of wish I'd stayed, in that case," she murmured.

He smirked, moving back a few steps to pick up his tea, watching her over the mug as he took a drink. The effect was kind of lost when his glasses fogged up, making her giggle. She couldn't believe she'd only seen him in glasses the one time before, when he'd been locked out of his flat.

"How come you never wear your glasses? Do you not really need them much?"

"Oh, no, my eyesight is terrible. I just wear my contacts."

"Easier?" she guessed.

"I mean, sort of, but I just don't think glasses suit me. You should see my school photos. I had these old-fashioned wire frames and braces for about two years. My mum's still got the photos up, at home. I keep begging her to take them down, but she won't."

"My mum's still got our baby photos around. There's like a shrine to us in the one cabinet, there's so many photos."

Jamie laughed.

"I think you're wrong, by the way. About glasses not suiting you. I think you look better in them. Not that you don't look good without them, but –"

"Are you trying to flirt with me, Eloise?"

"God, I hope not. If that's what passes for flirting ..." She puffed out her cheeks, shaking her head dramatically.

The mug clinked lightly as he set it back down, empty now. "Have you got any plans for today?"

"Er, I don't ... think so." Originally, her plans had involved watching half a dozen Christmas movies (including a marathon of all three *The Santa Clause* movies) and wrapping presents. She'd drive her parents' gifts down later in the week before they flew.

Now he'd mentioned it, she kind of hoped her plans for the day would involve the two of them, her bed, and no clothes.

"I need to do some last bits of shopping. Do you fancy coming with me? We could grab a coffee or something, or some lunch, if you fancy it. Not that you have to, or anything, and I wouldn't be offended, or anything, and I'm –"

Eloise smiled. Beamed, really. "I'd love to."

Nine days till Christmas

Chapter 9

The office was dead when she got in at three minutes past seven, except for Marcus. The light was on in his office. And it was so quiet she could hear him clacking at his keyboard, talking to himself quietly.

Cara dropped her bag at her desk. Her laptop and things were exactly where she'd left them on Friday before they'd set off to the party.

She could do this. She was a strong, independent woman (even if she had spent half her weekend overthinking George's weird phone call) and she could do this. She could face up to her mistakes.

She took the second coffee from the cardboard holder and crossed to Marcus' office, knocking on the door, opening it slowly when he said, "Come in." Cara tried to ignore how sick she felt. Her heart was beating so fast she was half-worried she'd keel over with cardiac arrest or something any second.

"Er, hi, it's just me. Not interrupting, am I?"

"Cara! No, of course not. Come on in. You're here early. Well – earlier than usual." He cracked a smile, pushing back from his desk and sweeping a hand at the chairs on the other side. She dithered, but stepped closer.

"I got you a coffee on my way in. Salted caramel latte."

"Oh, you star." He grinned, standing to reach for it. "This isn't a bribery coffee, is it? For Dave's job?"

"More like an apology coffee." Cara sat down now, so she could clamp her sweaty, shaking hands between her knees.

Marcus was easy and brilliant to work with, because he was so open and frank and friendly, and he didn't beat around the bush whenever there was any kind of bad news. Even if it was just that the milk had run out, so who wanted to go to the shop? Surely, if he was going to fire her or demote her or anything, he wouldn't be joking around with her.

But until she talked to him, that niggling doubt would eat her up.

Marcus opened his mouth, but she burst into her little speech before he got chance to talk.

"I'm so sorry for the way I behaved at the party on Friday. It was beyond unprofessional, and you have no idea how ashamed I am. I'm completely humiliated. And I'm not just saying that because there was kind of a chance I had a shot at Dave's job – I've never done *anything* so stupid or reckless or unprofessional in my life and I'm just so, so sorry, Marcus."

He raised his eyebrows when she finally stopped to catch her breath. He'd been listening with a serious expression, which wasn't doing anything to help.

"All done?"

She nodded, pursing her lips, cheeks on fire.

Marcus leaned forward and rested his elbows on his desk, hands open. "I bet you spent all weekend perfecting that, didn't you?"

"Only some of it. I was hungover for most of Saturday."

He laughed. "I'm not surprised! I'm more surprised you didn't end up in hospital getting your stomach pumped." She flushed even hotter. "But look, Cara, it was the Christmas party. Everyone gets a little too merry. This year you were just a bit … merrier than the rest of us. It's cool. It happens. But I really appreciate the apology. And the apology coffee."

"I just felt so awful about it. I shouldn't have let it happen. I should've been more sensible."

Marcus smiled, leaning back a little.

"And I know I won't be taking over from Dave now, after that, but I just wanted to say thank you for even considering me for it. I really appreciate it."

She started to stand, and Marcus shot to his feet so quickly she hesitated.

"You really think I'm not going to consider you for the job just because you got drunk at a party? You work harder than anyone else here – even me, sometimes, I think. I'd have to be mad to count you out."

"Oh." Now her heart was racing for a whole other reason, and her cheeks ached with the effort of not smiling. "Really? You're not just having me on?"

"Definitely not."

"Oh my God. Thank you. Thank you so much. You have no idea how much I appreciate it. Thank you. And, er, while I've got you – if you've got ten minutes, I just wanted to run something by you."

He turned his computer screen away from him.

"Shoot. I'm all ears."

"So I was thinking about how we could start an online book club. One book a fortnight. We write a review on it, maybe contact the author and see if they could do a mini interview – discuss it in a video ..."

She'd devoured one of the Christmas novels yesterday, been up until ten reading it – and so caught up she'd forgotten to make dinner, or even a cup of tea. Then she'd stayed awake till midnight brainstorming her new idea, planning out how they could really make it work.

"And they'd all be quick reads. Short books or books that are just easy to read and real page-turners. Maybe cheap on Kindle, or something, too. So people can read them on their commute and actually get through them, rather than just buying all these bestsellers and recommendations their friends make that just pile up because the idea of taking the time out to read a whole book is so intimidating."

Marcus nodded, sipping at his coffee, listening attentively. Cara could tell she'd got him hooked on the idea, from the way his eyes were wide and round, and how he'd leant right forward over the desk he was almost lying across it.

"Cara," he said, when she was done, "has anyone ever told you you're a genius?"

Most of the rest of the day, Cara was planning out her book club concept, pulling together documents on it, doing bits of research. She had her usual work to crack on with too – more than usual, since they'd taken most of Friday afternoon off for the party – but was too excited by her new idea to push it to the bottom of her to-do list. It'd never happen then, and Marcus wanted to get it kicked off in the New Year. Make a big push on having 'read more' as a resolution. He'd told her to pass some of her other work off to other people in the team – and she had handed over a few things, but Cara always felt weirdly protective of her workload.

She took a short break to catch up with Jen and gush about her new project – although that conversation did start with Jen scrunching up her face and saying, "Are you wearing a Christmas top?"

Cara looked down at her T-shirt with a snowman on,

one of many festive items of clothing she owned – and the first she'd worn all season. "Uh, yeah. And I've got my reindeer socks on."

"And are those – are you wearing snowman earrings too?"

"Why? What's wrong with them?"

Jen's face relaxed into a grin. "Nothing! Just – I didn't realise you got into Christmas quite so much. Sorry – you had something to tell me. Some new project?"

She was in the office working on it until seven before she even realised what time it was. And she only looked up then because one of the finance guys, who'd been putting in overtime for the approaching year-end, snapped off the lights in the rest of the office and bid her good-night.

"See you tomorrow," she said, blinking some life back into her dry eyes. She sat up, groaning, rolling her stiff neck around and cracking out her cramped fingers.

Cara clicked her phone, having ignored every buzz it made since her eighteen-minute lunch break (long enough to run down to a café, grab a coffee and sandwich and come back to scoff them at her desk). Some Instagram notifications, a couple of 'So-and-so tagged you in a comment' on Facebook, and two messages from George and dozens of texts from Eloise. Most of them were asking Cara to call her back; she had gossip and just had to talk to her. The rest were asking about Christmas plans.

Cara saved her documents, fired off a couple of last

emails and shut down her laptop for the day. Then she rang George.

"Cara! How are you?"

He sounded so happy to hear from her. He couldn't be cheating, could he? Nobody that sweet could be cheating. Not someone like George.

"Busy, as per. I got caught up reading last night when you rang, so I missed your call and just totally forgot to ring back."

"That's alright. Reading anything good?"

"Uh, only the cheesiest, cutest book about ex-lovers reunited at a Christmas market."

He laughed. "Well, sounds like you've recovered from your hangover now, at least."

Ooh, he was too sweet. There was no way he was cheating. There was some perfectly good, totally reasonable explanation.

"Yeah. And, thanks again, for – you know, taking care of me on Friday. You didn't have to come out and take me home, or stay to keep an eye on me."

"I didn't mind." She could hear the smile in his voice and relaxed into her seat, tucking one leg up and wrapping her arm around it. "How was work? Not too awkward?"

"Lots of people joking about the state I got into," she admitted, "but no, actually, it was a really great day." She explained, hearing the excitement build in her voice the more she talked about the book club idea.

"Are you still there now?"

"Yeah."

"I'm just on my way to the Tube. Do you want to meet for dinner somewhere?"

The way her heart flip-flopped was answer enough. "I've got an email voucher for Wagamama?"

"Sounds perfect."

They debated for a minute about which one to go to, before settling on one about halfway between their homes. Cara was already on her way out of the door when they said goodbye.

She should probably call Eloise back. Later, she decided. She'd lose signal in a minute when she was on the Underground.

Probably, she should go to Eloise for Christmas. She had Christmas Day and Boxing Day off. She could switch her bus ticket, travel up in the evening on Christmas Eve. Come back down Boxing Day. Probably take her laptop up to do a bit of work.

Most of the office were taking the Friday off too, since it was the day after Boxing Day. She couldn't blame them. Last year she'd done the same. But she had so much to do. Especially now she had the whole book club thing to sort out. She couldn't afford to take any time off right now.

It made more sense for her to travel. Eloise would want to take over the cooking anyway and, also, Eloise's flat was way warmer than Cara's house. And the only decorations they had were a small tree that had cost them five quid and some baubles from the pound shop. Extravagant.

Eloise's flat would be like bloody Lapland. Except warmer.

A huge part of her was resistant though. Eloise had two whole weeks off work, and she wouldn't have any work to do over the Christmas break. And she had a car – it'd be easier for her to travel really and cheaper, probably, than it would be for Cara to take the train or even a bus. So why couldn't Eloise be the one to come to her?

And why did she have to make such a bloody fuss? Didn't she understand how difficult Cara was finding it to balance everything right now without throwing a few days away for Christmas into the mix?

Arriving at the restaurant and seeing George waiting outside was enough to distract her. He'd loosened his tie, undone his top two shirt buttons, and his hair was a little rumpled like he'd been pushing it around while he worked. It looked adorable.

She matched his beaming smile as she got closer and kissed him briefly on the lips. "Alright?"

"Better now." He winked, making her giggle.

She was crazy to ever think he might be cheating on her, right?

George left his phone on the table when he went to the bathroom.

It buzzed.

Instinctively, Cara's eyes flicked up. When she saw it wasn't her phone, her eyes drifted to his.

The green text icon.

Lina.

Cara's whole body seemed to burn up, catch fire, her eyes bulging.

The notification faded away, the screen darkening, but then another text came through. Lina again.

Cara glanced towards the bathroom. She'd see him coming. She was only curious. She was just ... She wasn't doing anything wrong, was she? It wasn't like she was going through his phone. She just happened to see his notifications.

She just happened to twirl the phone to face her, clicking the screen on.

Are you around tonight? Could you pop round? I've got some new ...

I've got popcorn too. Toffee. Your faaaaaave

Cara wondered what the rest of the first message said. New what? *New what?*

New underwear to show off, her brain filled in, *because this is some girl he's cheating on you with, and that's why he's not mentioned her once tonight, even though he probably spent the whole weekend with her. Whoever she is.*

It didn't matter how logical she tried to be about it; she couldn't shake the fact that he hadn't told her about this girl, and that gave her enough doubt that rationality was a thing of the past. Josh had never told Eloise about Alyssa, and look what happened there.

Cara twisted the phone back to the way it was before and sat back. Should she confront him?

Of course, if she was wrong – she might ruin everything.

But if she wasn't, he'd already ruined everything, and at least she could get out before it was too late.

So, she had to ask him. Just get a straight answer out of him. Say she'd seen the texts, wondered who Lina was. It didn't have to sound like a big deal.

But when George sat back down a minute or two later, all smiles, offering her a bite of his food because he knew she'd been eyeing it up since it arrived, something stopped her asking. She could hear how frosty her replies suddenly became as they talked.

That same something stopped her asking when they kissed goodbye back by the Tube station and made her kiss him on the cheek instead of the lips.

Maybe it was already too late.

Cara felt like she'd already fallen for him, utterly and completely.

Seven days till Christmas

Chapter 10

That was it.

One week until Christmas. That meant there was only six sleeps to go.

They couldn't put this off any longer.

She'd sent enough bloody texts and Snapchats and Facebook and WhatsApp messages to Cara over the last few days that she was sick of being ignored. Time for an ambush.

Eloise was shocked when Cara answered her phone at six twenty-three a.m. – she'd half expected her to already be on her way to work, if not already there. But, judging by the room behind her sister's face on the video, Cara was still at home. Her make-up was half done – there were stripes on her face where she'd not yet blended. She was wearing huge dangly candy-cane earrings.

Eloise couldn't even laugh at the sight and screenshot it.

"We need to talk."

"Oh, God, that sounds serious," Cara joked as she propped her device up to balance somewhere while she turned back to the mirror, grabbing up a sponge to blend her make-up in. "Wait, is this about that Jamie? I told you I'd call you back; I've just been so busy, sorry. You won't believe what happened in work. So I went out to the shops on Sunday, and –"

"Shut up a minute," Eloise snapped, because this was stressing her out way too much. Of course she wanted to hear what happened in Cara's work and of course she wanted to know what she was so excited about, and she wanted to tell her all about her last-minute day out with Jamie.

But this was *Christmas*.

The rest could wait.

Cara stopped talking, mouth hanging open. She blinked at the screen, mouth closing slowly, and waited.

"What are we doing next week?"

"For what?"

Oh my God, she's got to be kidding me. She doesn't know. She's forgotten. She's actually so busy in work she doesn't even know.

Eloise tried hard not to scream.

"For Christmas. God. Cara, I've cut you some slack here because I know how stressed out you've been at work, but

I need to know. I need to know what to do about food, and when you'll be here, and –"

"Oh, er, well ... I could come up Christmas Day. Travel up in the morning, like I was going to do originally. And then I was thinking I'd come back on Boxing Day. And you don't need to worry about food – we could just do, like, turkey sandwiches or something? Buy some of that pre-packaged stuff. Get a bit of cranberry sauce."

"You don't even want Christmas dinner?"

"I'm not that bothered. I'm just saying. It'll be easier for you."

Cheaper, was what Eloise heard, that Cara didn't say.

"It's a lot of fuss, when it's just the two of us."

"Well, what time are you going back on Boxing Day? We'll have almost all day to eat the leftovers. I can just do two lots of Christmas dinner. It's not like Dad doesn't usually do that on Boxing Day, when the turkey's big enough."

"Oh. Um." Cara leant away from the camera, doing her mascara now. "I thought I'd come back early morning. I'll have chance to get some work done, that way, and I can get out from under your feet."

You won't be under my feet. It's Christmas. Time for family. I want you around. I miss you.

But what she said was, "You're working on Boxing Day? It's a bank holiday. Your boss can't make you –"

"He's not. We're not working. I've just got a ton of stuff to do before the New Year."

"Can't you do it here? You could work from here on the Friday too, stay the whole weekend. I'll put on a big buffet, like Mum and Dad do for New Year. You could invite George to come up."

"Oh, God, don't even talk to me about George. So, you know that girl, Lina, he mentioned? Well, last night –"

"No. No tangents! I promise I want to hear all about this, but not right now. So what you're telling me is – you're spending maybe six hours with me on Christmas Day, don't want to do a turkey dinner, you'll be rushing off early the next day, and I'm not going to see you again until who knows when?"

Cara at least had the good grace to look away, blushing through her make-up.

"You realise how awful that is, don't you? Making me spend the holidays alone? It's your fault Mum and Dad are going away. I don't have Josh to spend it with this year. None of our mates live near for me to crash their day. And now –"

"Not everything's about you, El! If you're that upset about it, come stay at mine, and stay until you have to go back to school. You can explore the city a bit while I'm in work, or –"

"What, so I can mooch around on my own while you work? No, thanks."

"Fine. But I don't hear you offering a solution."

"I did! And you wouldn't have it! You want to work non-stop? Fine. Go ahead, Ebenezer. See if I give a damn."

Eloise hit the red hang-up button so furiously she missed. Had to stab at it a few times while Cara protested weakly on her end, before she cut off altogether. She left the phone on the kitchen counter, resolutely ignoring the sound of Cara calling her back.

If Cara was going to be so bloody-minded, then fine. See if she cared. It wasn't like they'd not seen each other in months. It wasn't like Christmas was always the one time she got to stop competing with their friends for Cara's attention. It wasn't like she wasn't already so used to spending time by herself and missing home.

It was only afterwards that she realised they'd never got to gossip about the guys in their lives. And she really wanted to know what the hell was going on with George and this Lina character, whoever she was.

The morning went on *forever*. They were putting on their first performance of the nativity that afternoon, with the infants year groups – which, of course, meant hours of trying to calm down children, reassure the ones who were crying that they didn't want to perform and fix a few tears in costumes.

Oh, and try to fix the props, when the 2D cut-out stand of a stable fell over and cracked in two.

Eloise had never been so glad to see lunchtime.

She was sick of hearing about Mary and Joseph and the shepherds watching their flock by night. She was sick of hearing those same bloody songs all over again. She was sick of hearing all the children chat about what they'd asked Santa for this year and what they'd be doing with their families for the holidays.

She was sick of hearing about bloody Christmas.

A few of the other teachers had taken charge of putting out chairs ready for the afternoon's performance, giving Eloise and Mrs Abbott – Abigail – a chance to sit down with a cup of tea at long last. Abigail had even managed to procure one of the boxes of Roses from the staffroom.

"We need it more than they do," she'd announced, dropping the box onto the table between them. They'd holed themselves away in Eloise's classroom for some peace and quiet, at least for the next half hour.

"You're a gem." Ignoring her sandwich, she reached for one of the caramels. She was in desperate need of tea and chocolates right now. The sandwich could wait.

"What are you so grumpy about today?" Abigail asked. "Get up on the wrong side of bed? Realised you forgot to buy for someone?"

"I don't think my sister's coming for Christmas."

"But – why not? Did she decide to go away with your parents? Going to her boyfriend's?"

"I don't know that George is her boyfriend," Eloise muttered. Then, "But no. She's just too busy working. Honestly. Honest to God, that's why. Because she wants to *work*. She doesn't even have to. She can take holiday. She can work remotely too, when she has to! And she won't! She's even going to work on Boxing Day."

"They can't make her do that, surely," Abigail said.

"They're not. She just *wants* to."

"Did you do something to piss her off? Maybe that's why she doesn't want to come. Work's just an outlet or an excuse or something." Abigail spoke with such calm, wise tones. She had two kids around Eloise's own age. Sometimes they'd gossip like good friends and then, times like this, Eloise felt like she was chatting to her mum.

"No, she's just being miserable. I know she's a workaholic and it's great that she loves her job so much, but ... it's Christmas, you know? It's different. She used to love Christmas. Like me. She got a group of us to go carolling at uni. Do you know how hard it is to get uni students to go properly carolling without a few drinks? And now all she wants to do is push her way up the corporate ladder."

"I'm sure it's not like that," Abigail soothed. She rifled through the box of Roses for another caramel one, pushing it towards Eloise.

"She doesn't even want Christmas dinner."

"Alright, *now* I'm convinced."

"I know, right?" Eloise vented a while longer, pulling her sandwich apart while she talked, the minutes slipping by. Her tea was barely warm when she started to run out of steam.

She took a long drink of it, draining the cup, and sighed, pushing her knuckles into her forehead. She'd have to dig the paracetamol out of her bag. And the ibuprofen too, maybe.

"Well, you're always welcome round ours for Christmas," Abigail said, smiling. "You'd get on with my kids. Amber's always going on about that *Thrones* show."

"Oh, God, thank you, but – I couldn't intrude like that. Christmas is for family."

"Exactly. And it's not a time to sit in front of the telly watching whatever crap is on until the *EastEnders* special all by yourself." Abigail patted her hand, in full mum-mode now. "I'd hate to think of you all alone like that on Christmas."

Eloise didn't know what to say. She was so overwhelmed that Abigail would even offer. She didn't think people really did that.

She was *this close* to just bursting into tears. Abigail seemed to notice, because she gave her a moment to gulp down the lump in her throat.

"Think about it," Abigail went on. "Even if it gets to Christmas Day morning and you change your mind. We'll have so much food you'll be doing us a favour if we need to make you up a plate."

"Thank you," Eloise choked out, but the words didn't seem like enough.

"Enough moaning about your workaholic sister," Abigail said, digging around the Roses box for one she liked. "I want to hear more about that neighbour of yours. I love a good gossip about boys, and you're about the only one here I get to do that with. My Amber won't talk to me about anything like that. Have you seen him since Sunday?"

"Only a little," she laughed. "We've texted a bit. He was out with people last night, and I had some lesson plans to sort out. He's planning to go home for Christmas, but we might do something this weekend. Another proper date. Not just hanging out in one of our flats with takeaway. I feel like that's not much of a date when he only lives opposite."

"Ooh! Where do you think you'll go? Is he around for New Year? That'd be nice, if you can go out somewhere with him. Guaranteed a kiss at midnight then, aren't you?" Abigail winked at her, leaving Eloise to pull a face and roll her eyes.

"Oh, leave off! But honestly, I've no idea. I haven't asked him yet. Do you want more tea? We might not get chance this afternoon."

Eloise checked her phone once the nativity was finally underway. Other teachers were looking on and ready to prompt the children. She was 'backstage' – also known as Abigail's classroom – waiting with some of the children, and Damien, one of the TAs.

She had like, a million texts and missed calls from Cara. Lots from their parents too.

Scrolling through them, her dad was obviously on her side. Cara should take some time off work, she really needed to, but she could at least compromise and work from Eloise's for a few days – surely her boss wouldn't mind that.

Their mum, however, was siding with Cara.

It's good that your sister's working so hard for this promotion. We need to support her! She's always been such a hard worker. She's under enough stress, why don't you drive down to her? You've got much longer off work and I'm sure she'd really appreciate it. You could go back on the weekend then. Have a couple of days in London – I'm sure Cara would get out in the evenings with you for some drinks or the cinema! She'll need a bit of a break.

Try not to be too hard on your sister, sweetie. I know it's hard but she's putting so much into this job and she's got a real shot at this promotion! You'd be doing her a big favour if you went to her for Christmas.

You really need to sort this out with Cara so you can sort out buying some food. Dad's suggested maybe you could get takeaway! Save you both cooking LOL

Are you still coming over this weekend? I'm doing a curry

Eloise replied to her mum's most recent text that yes, she was still coming over, then stepped out to call Cara.

Straight to voicemail.

"Cara, it's me. Look, I know how much this promotion means to you, but you really need to take a break. It's Christmas. And I really don't want to spend it alone. Dave and Marcus aren't even expecting you to work, so I'm sure you can work from mine, even if it's just on Boxing Day. You can invite George up if you like, as well. The more the merrier. I'll do all the turkey dinner for us, and the flat's all decorated. I've got all your presents under the tree ready. Please, Cara, just – come for Christmas."

Five days till Christmas

Chapter 11

"Don't you fancy coming home for the weekend?"

"Of course I do, Mum, but it's just mad here. You got all your presents, didn't you?"

"Yes, but that's not ..." Her mum trailed off with a sigh and Cara was glad they weren't on video chat. She'd called her mum while she was on the walk back to her house, having had to take a different route due to 'essential maintenance works' on her usual Tube home. "It'd be lovely to have you here. This'll be the only time we're all together until the New Year. Eloise hasn't said anything, but I know she's feeling very down about Christmas being a bit different this year."

"I'll see, Mum, but I don't know."

"Are you working this weekend?"

"A bit."

A lot.

She really needed this book club idea to be a success. She knew it wouldn't have a huge bearing on whether she got the promotion or not – they'd need to hire someone before the book club even had chance to really take off – but still. This was a project she was driving completely. Marcus had more or less given her free rein on it, with Cara only asking opinions and input and feedback. She wasn't reporting to anybody on this. She had real responsibility here.

And she loved her job. Especially this project. So what was the big deal if she wanted to spend some of her weekend working? Her dad didn't really get it, but her mum did.

She felt like it said something that even her mum wanted her to take a break, though.

"Well, try and come up, love. We'd like to see you before we go away. And you and Eloise will have chance to raid my cupboards then, if there's anything you need for Christmas Day. Did you get my email about the travel over Christmas, by the way? Eloise said you're probably going up to her. I sent you a link about all the travel services that aren't running or will be disrupted ..."

While her mum told her about the National Rail services she didn't plan to take anyway, Cara tried not to feel too guilty. Eloise might have successfully guilted her into travelling up for Christmas Day, but she hadn't really planned on going to see her parents this weekend.

She knew she should.

She kind of wanted to.

But ... *work*. And the last-minute travel – especially at this time of year – would cost her a fortune. And it wasn't like she wouldn't see them some time in January, anyway, when she went home for her dad's birthday.

"I'll try and make it," she told her mum when the conversation started to wrap up, "but I'm not making any promises."

Cara had barely hung up when her phone began to buzz again.

George.

She'd text him during the week, but they hadn't called like they usually would, and she'd not seen him since Monday. That wasn't unusual in itself, but she knew she was avoiding him. She'd ignored a few of his messages. He'd asked if she was home so he could pop over to see her for a while last night. She had been home, doing more research for the book club that could've waited until the morning, but told him she was busy.

She'd talked to her housemates about it too, because she hadn't been able to help herself. Henry thought she was overreacting; Elliot and Laurie said he was almost certainly cheating, and Jamilla had declared she'd always known that boy was too good to be true and that Cara was too good for him anyway.

None of which were helpful, ultimately.

The phone kept ringing.

She wanted to talk to him. She wanted to see him. There was that ball of butterflies in her stomach and she wanted to answer the phone and hear him ask if she wanted to do something tonight, if she had plans or if he could see her.

But there was that little nagging doubt prodding at her that said he was only calling because he was going to break up with her because of this Lina. Whoever she was.

She answered anyway.

"I've been trying to get through to you for ages! Not ignoring me, are you?"

"I was on the phone to my mum."

"Don't suppose you fancy doing something tonight? Have a quiet night in? I bet all the restaurants will be packed, seeing as it's the last Friday before Christmas. All those office parties and stuff. I'll cook? I can come to yours, if that's easier for you?"

He barely let her get a word in edgeways. He just sounded so hyped at the thought of seeing her. He was so sweet like that.

But – Lina.

She couldn't keep going in circles like this. It was already driving her insane. Cara pursed her lips to herself, resolute. She'd have it out with him. She'd get this over and done with right now.

Then, at least, she'd know if she should return his Christmas present or not.

And whether she had to get over him or not.

"I'll come to yours," she said. At least, that way, she could leave. Storm out, if he was cheating. But she'd be more in control of the situation then. It'd make everything easier. "I just need to drop all my stuff off at home and then I'll come over."

"Brilliant. What about a curry? How does that sound? Or do you fancy something else?"

"Er, whatever. I don't mind. You pick."

She might not even be eating it anyway.

Agonising over whether she should get changed or not, Cara yanked the brush through her hair. It was tangled from the walk home and the wind. She put on some more deodorant and perfume, slapped on a little more powder to freshen up her face, and left it there.

No point in getting all dressed up for a break-up, right?

And if there was another explanation, well, George wouldn't care. He'd looked after her drunk. He'd seen her in a worse state.

But she still agonised over it, and rang Eloise.

Eloise answered the FaceTime call and it took a few seconds to connect. There was no video, but she could hear Eloise giggling, squealing, "Stop it! Go make me some tea!"

When it connected, her sister's face was flushed, eyes bright, smile wide. She looked happier than she'd looked to see Cara calling in weeks. "Hiya. Alright?"

"Is Jamie there?"

"What? No. Why would you think that?"

"Can I open the shortbread?" a guy – Jamie, presumably – yelled from somewhere in the background. Eloise turned away from the camera.

"No, you can't! They're for Christmas!"

"What about the After Eights?"

"No! There's some custard creams open somewhere. They're probably still alright." She blushed when she looked back at Cara. "Okay, you caught me."

Cara so didn't need this right now. She wished Jamie weren't there.

It wasn't like she wasn't happy for Eloise. After all that had happened with that arsehole Josh, she was glad her sister had found someone she really liked. (And Cara knew their parents would be happy it wasn't some random bloke she'd met online.)

But right now, it felt like salt in the wound.

Eloise seemed to notice something was wrong, sitting up straighter on the sofa and muting her TV, bringing the camera closer to her face. "What's up? What's the matter? Don't tell me you're cancelling Christmas again and decided not to come at all."

"No, it's not that."

"Mum and Dad said you're not coming home this weekend. You should, you know. They miss you. And it might do you some good, to have a –"

"I don't need a break," she snapped, jaw clenched. "And will you shut up about me coming home? Do you have any idea how needy you sound? Coming home isn't going to help any of this. And that's not even why I *called*."

Eloise sat up straighter, blinking at the screen. Cara repressed a groan. Great. Just what she needed. To have made Eloise cry.

But she gulped, and said shakily, "Oh, right."

"Sorry," Cara said stiffly. "I didn't mean to shout. It's just that I'm going to see George."

"Oh." Her sister perked up a little, writing off the near-miss of an argument. "Right. And …?"

"I'm going to ask him about Lina."

Eloise's face said *At last!* but she composed herself quickly, and what she said out loud was, "Oh, sweetie. I mean, there could be a totally good explanation for it."

"Like what?"

"Like … she's … an ex he's stayed friends with and other girlfriends think that's weird and they break up with him over it. Ex-wife – he got married when he was like, sixteen, divorced three months later, and he's too embarrassed to talk about it. She's his parole officer and he was done for … um … insider trading. Er … It's his boss."

"His boss who texts him to come over and she's got his favourite flavour popcorn?"

"Exactly. It sounds bad when you say it like that, which is why he's not told you."

Cara rolled her eyes.

She'd been over every conceivable explanation that sounded at least halfway plausible, and none of them seemed to make any sense to her. Eloise was only trying to help, she knew, but she wasn't doing a great job of making her feel better.

"Where are you meeting him?"

"I'm going to his. He's planning to cook dinner."

"Aww," Eloise cooed, sympathetic expression melting as if she'd just seen a cute dog. "See? That's sweet. Josh would never have done that for me. Cara, I just feel like he's too sweet to be a cheat."

"Who's a cheat?" Jamie, again, in the background. Cara saw Eloise take hold of a cup of tea, pulling it near her chest.

"We don't know yet," her sister said. She turned the camera on Jamie, and Cara was kind of surprised. He didn't strike her as Eloise's type. He was kind of – well, *rugged*, was the only word Cara could think of. Scruffy hair, stubble. He didn't look anything like Josh. Or any of the other guys Eloise had been on dates with.

(Cara had no confidence in online dating and had made Eloise send her pictures and names of all the guys she'd gone on a date with from Tinder. Just in case. Their mum sent them a lot of horror-story news links about that kind of stuff.)

"Hiya," he said, smiling, waving to the camera.

"Hey," she replied, smiling back. "Er, Miss Elizabeth?" Eloise turned the camera back on her.

"Much as I'd like to properly meet your Mr Darcy –"

"*Funny*."

"– I've got to go in a minute."

"Right. Sorry. That's good, though, that you're going to his. You can leave if you have to break up with him."

"That's what I thought."

"Okay. Well, let me know, as soon as you know? Call me if you need me. Or even if it's all okay, call me. I need to know who this Lina is too."

"I will."

George was beaming when he opened the door. A tuft of hair was sticking up from his otherwise neat look, the sleeves of his shirt rolled up just past his elbows and a plastic apron tied around him, splattered with bits of sauce.

"Come in, come in, you're letting the cold in."

He shared a ground-floor flat with two other guys. George's room was more the size of a bathroom than a bedroom; he could only fit a single bed in it, which was why they spent more time at hers.

But she was always surprised how clean the place was. A little messy, maybe, with shoes and bags and phone chargers scattered around, but clean. It smelled delightful too – a Balti curry smell wafted down the hallway from the kitchen, and she was sure that was some garlic and coriander naan bread she could smell too. Her favourite, as he well knew. Her stomach growled.

George moved forward to kiss her before she took off her coat and shoes, and she turned her head to the side, brushing it off with a smile.

"Your housemates not in?"

"Tom's been drinking since about ten this morning with some of his mates from school, and Gary's just left for his work Christmas party."

Probably for the best. She was so wired and on edge right now this might turn into a screaming match.

George was back in the kitchen, stirring a pot with a wooden spoon, by the time she'd taken off her coat and shoes. It wasn't that she was staying (probably), but she knew they always took their shoes off in the flat.

"I need to talk to you."

"What was that?"

He had the fan on over the stove, and music playing, and the window open with the wind howling outside.

Cara tried again, wringing her fingers. "I need to talk to you."

George looked at her for a long moment – her big eyes, downturned mouth pinched thin, worrying hands – and turned the heat on the stove down, snapping the fan off and stepping towards her. "What's the matter?"

Why did she feel like *she* was the one doing something wrong?

This was like the one and only time she'd missed a lecture. She'd slept in too late, knew she wouldn't make it in time, and decided, just that once, she wouldn't go. She'd felt sick with nerves for the whole next hour, and two days later when she'd walked into the next lecture with the same professor. Like she'd be scolded for missing one and sent to the headmaster, where they'd ring her parents and threaten to expel her. And universities didn't even *have* headmasters.

"I have to ask you something. And I just need an honest answer. I don't want ... I don't want, like, excuses, or anything, or ... I just want the truth. Okay?"

"Okay ..." He dragged the word out, frowning.

It felt like it took her an age to spit the words out, but finally she did.

"Who's Lina?"

George looked so taken aback that for a second she felt like a total idiot. Then she realised maybe it was just that he thought he'd done such a good job of covering his tracks and clenched her jaw, resolute. He turned to the stove again, twisting the knobs and turning everything off.

"I heard you on the phone last weekend," she explained, not even sure why she felt like she needed to explain herself. That was what he should be doing. "And she text you the other night, when we went out to dinner. I wasn't snooping. I just saw the notifications come up."

George was nodding, looking somewhere by her feet, and she waited, trying to stop her breathing sounding so loud and ragged, until he looked up.

"Did you think I was cheating on you?"

That's just not an answer, is it?

"Who is she?"

"Can I get you a drink?" He was moving towards the fridge now.

"*George.*"

He stopped moving and looked back at her.

"Is this why you've been so off with me, pushing me away, ignoring my messages?"

"I have *not* –"

"Yes, you have. You know you have. And I couldn't work out what the hell I'd done so wrong that you sounded so pissed off when you did deign to speak to me."

Cara glowered at him. How dare he act like she was the one in the wrong here? How dare he? What fucking right did he have to talk to her like that, when he was the one who'd been lying to her, hiding some *girl* from her?

"Who's Lina, George?"

His shoulders drooped. He turned away. He sighed.

"She's my sister."

"But ... you don't have a sister," she said warily. She gulped. "And if that's the best excuse you can come up with ..."

"It's not an excuse. It's ... a weird topic to talk about. I never know how to bring it up."

Cara looked at him like he'd just grown a second head.

"Our parents split up when we were little. My mum moved back up to Yorkshire, near her family, with my sister. I saw them maybe twice a year. We didn't talk much, growing up. It probably didn't help that she went to university in Australia. She's a few years older than me."

Cara kept staring at him.

"She's been in hospital. She's been travelling, and just got back. She went to see my dad and got in a car accident. She's fine, pretty much. Broken leg, few bruises. I went to visit her last weekend. That's where I was. We've been talking more since, 'cause … I don't know. Just makes you realise, I guess, when something like that happens. It could've been a lot worse. She was lucky. And she was trying really hard to build bridges with our dad … It's not like we had a big fight and that's why we never talked, but yeah, that's what the phone call and the texts were all about."

Oh, God. Oh, *God*.

Eloise was right.

He'd pulled a Jude Law from *The Holiday* on her. There *was* an explanation. A good one. A really, really bloody *good* one.

An estranged sister in a car accident hadn't even cropped up as an idea when she'd been thinking about it. It never would've occurred to her in a million years.

And all she had to say was:

"Oh, my God."

Because she was *such* an idiot. She was so stupid.

"My dad and step-mum are going to cancel their holiday. My mum's been down and is staying with them for now too, just till Lina's out of hospital. They're planning to stay through the holidays. Play happy families and all that."

"Are you not spending Christmas in the city any more then?"

She had a thousand and one questions, but that one seemed like a safe one to ask.

"I'll probably just go back for Christmas Day and Boxing Day."

She nodded.

It all made so much sense now. His dad lived just near Bromley, which wasn't that far away. He could do that visit in an evening. It'd mean a late night or an early start, but it was doable. He could've gone to visit the other evening when Lina text him while they were at dinner. He definitely could've gone to visit last Saturday, when he'd dashed off.

"You thought I was cheating, didn't you?"

She squirmed. "A little. I mean, you've *got* to admit – it looked suspicious. I figured if she was a mate or family, you'd have mentioned it. It was only dodgy because you didn't. And it's not like I was *trying* to snoop. I figured there had to be a reason why you were hiding it from me, why you never mentioned her."

"And cheating is the most obvious reason, let's be fair."

Cara cringed, biting her lip – but George smiled a little. He wasn't pissed off, at least. She wouldn't have blamed him if he had been.

"I bet Eloise thought I was too."

"She thought Lina was your kid."

George let out a laugh at that – the big, belly kind, and she relaxed, leaning against the doorframe and letting her hands stop fidgeting. He reached for the oven knobs again, then cast her a sidelong glance. "You still staying for dinner?"

"Damn right I am. This smells bloody gorgeous, and I'm starving. Shall I get some plates out?"

She helped with the last bit of the cooking – pouring drinks, draining the rice, and George told her more about his sister. She was twenty-nine, a freelance journalist, travelled abroad a lot. Lina (which, apparently, was short for Paulina – they were both named after grandparents on different sides of the family) was a huge reader, keeping up a book blog in her spare time, though it had fallen by the wayside in the last few months, and was really into astrology.

"Okay, this might sound ... presumptuous," Cara said, taking a chance, tearing some naan bread apart to dip into her curry, "but you think she'd be able to help me out with this book club thing at work? Even if it's just recommending a couple of books or something ..."

"Are you kidding? She'd love that. She was meant to go on some hiking holiday for her next article, but she can't now, because of her leg. She'll be looking for another project to get stuck into, take her mind off it."

"Are you sure? It's just ... I don't want to, like, bother her or anything." Cara chewed her food, buying time, before deciding to just confess. "And I don't want to step on toes or anything, if you're still ... getting to know each other a bit more, or whatever."

"It's alright. It's not like we never talked before; we just weren't that close. She was more like one of those cousins you know about but just don't see much. That's why I don't talk about her with new people I meet. The whole situation is a bit *Parent Trap* when you say it out loud."

Cara squinted, tilted her head, then snapped her fingers. "Of course! Lindsay Lohan! That's who you remind me of!"

"I should've told you, though. I should've said something when she went into hospital. I didn't know how to bring it up. It sounds a bit weird if I just suddenly announce I've got a sister I never mentioned, totally out of the blue, when we've been talking for – what, months, now."

"Talking? Gosh. There's a reality check. Here I thought we said we were in a relationship. Didn't we say we were eloping in Vegas at New Year?"

George wagged his fork at her. "You're right. I'm so sorry. I'm a terrible fiancé to have already forgotten our upcoming nuptials."

"But seriously," Cara said, dropping her knife to reach and squeeze his hand, "I get why you didn't say anything. And I'm sorry if I made things awkward by jumping to conclusions."

"You didn't. I feel like a crappy boyfriend for making you think I was cheating."

"'Tis the season for forgiving, right?"

"Something like that." He grinned back, eyes sparkling.

She was so glad there was an explanation. She was so glad he wasn't cheating.

Because she suddenly realised she was so, *so* in love with him.

132

Four days till Christmas

Chapter 12

A knock on the door. Eloise looked at her mum. "Are you expecting anyone?"

"Probably the post. You know what your dad's like, always ordering stuff on Amazon. Go get it, will you, love?"

She left her mum rolling clothes up ready to be packed in the suitcase and ran down to answer the door. Someone was singing outside – *Away in a Manger*. It was a little early for carol singers, she thought.

Eloise unlocked the door, opening it wide, assuming it'd be some of the neighbours popping round with a Christmas card or something. But her mouth dropped open, jaw hitting the floor, gawping at the people on the doorstep.

Cara stopped singing long enough to erupt into giggles, throwing her arms around her. "Surprise!"

Eloise floundered for words, eventually managing to hug her twin back. "What are you doing here? What – Dad? You knew about this?"

He said he'd gone out for more milk, and she'd thought it was weird because they had plenty of milk, and they were due to fly the next day, but she'd just assumed it was a cover for something like: *I've forgotten to buy part of one of your presents and need to cover my tracks so it doesn't look like I'm rubbish at this.*

She'd *never*, not in a million years, thought he'd be bringing Cara home.

"What's going on? I don't ... What're you doing here?"

"It's the last chance we'll all get to spend time together before Christmas," Cara chirped, like it was obvious, like she hadn't been a complete and utter Grinch about the holidays for the past several weeks. "So I got an early bus up, and a train, and Dad picked me up from the station."

Eloise squealed, hugging Cara tighter. "I didn't think you'd come!"

"What can I say? I'm in a good mood. The sun is shining –"

"It's barely two degrees outside."

"– and you were right about George having a good explanation, and I managed to find a cheap last-minute deal on the bus service."

Eloise laughed. That was more like the Cara she knew.

"Oh my God. Okay. Go say hi to Mum and then come and tell me everything. I can't believe you didn't call me last night." She glanced then at Cara's backpack, and at their dad, who wasn't holding any other luggage. "You're not staying?"

"The bus back is at five. I'm here most of the day. It's not even lunchtime yet."

"I meant until Christmas. You could've just come and stayed at mine."

Cara waved a hand. "I have work."

"You're mad."

"We can't all have cushy term-time only jobs."

Eloise narrowed her eyes, hands on her hips. "Say that again and I might have to uninvite you for Christmas."

Cara was already making her way upstairs to see their mum, though, and Eloise turned to her dad as he shut the door.

"This is Mum's fault," she told him. "Encouraging her to work hard. What kind of parent is she?"

"Clearly, a dreadful one, given that Cara's almost definitely got that promotion after being there less than two years." He grinned and hung his coat on the end of the stairs. Eloise tried not to read too much into that and take it as: *Your sister is already up for promotion, and what have you been doing?* "Do you want a mince pie? I hid a box from your mum and there's two left. Bet we can scoff them before they come back downstairs."

"Ooh. Go on then."

Eloise had fully expected to be in for a grilling about Jamie, having casually mentioned their one single actual, proper date to her mum on the phone, but with Cara there too there was no escape from the Spanish Inquisition. She made sure Cara had it just as bad, though, joining in with her parents and peppering her with questions about George.

She spared her sister talking about whoever that Lina girl was until they were doing the washing-up after dinner, leaving their parents to do some more packing. They could hear them bickering upstairs about how much sun cream to take, or if their dad had packed enough underpants (eight couldn't possibly be enough, he declared, even if they would be in their swimming costumes almost the whole time – and had he picked up the travel wash? Had he wrapped it in clingfilm in case it leaked? *Properly?*). Eloise plugged her phone into the speaker in the kitchen, playing Michael Bublé's Christmas album to drown out their parents.

"So," she said, wiping the bubbles off a plate and handing it to Cara, "who was she?"

"What? Who?"

"Lina! You know, the girl you were going insane over, convinced your boyfriend was cheating on you? That *she*. I'm guessing there was a bloody good explanation, since you didn't ring me or text me, and you showed up here all smiles and all, 'Ooh, George this!' and 'George that!'"

Cara's cheeks turned a little pink. "So maybe you were right."

"And?"

"She's his sister."

"Right. Hang on. I'm going to need a much better explanation than that. Nobody just has a secret sibling they never talk about for no good reason."

Cara sighed, and explained how George and his sister had grown up apart and reconnected recently after she'd been in a car accident.

"I just felt so awful, standing there all ready to yell at him for cheating on me or using me or whatever, and he felt bad because he'd made it look like I couldn't trust him by not just telling me about her, and ... Oh, God, it was such a mess."

"I mean, I did tell you."

"Don't even."

Eloise grinned at the washing-up bowl, scrubbing her lipstick off a glass. "But you're all sorted now?"

"We are."

Glancing sideways, she saw the huge grin stretching ear-to-ear across Cara's face, and laughed. "Go on. How many times?"

"I don't know what you're talking about."

"You *shlaaaaaag*."

"At least I'm in a relationship."

"Oh, boo. Don't be so traditional. This isn't the fifties."

"So what are you and Jamie doing anyway? I know you told Mum it was only the one proper date, and it's still early days but – seriously, what's happening there?"

"I have absolutely no idea."

So maybe she'd spent a lot of time with Jamie – especially this week. And yes, they'd slept together, and they'd had that adorable date together on Sunday, mooching around the shops and talking nonstop and drinking hot chocolates and she'd even convinced him to take a spin on the ice skating rink in town. She *might* have bragged to Cara about it afterwards that at least neither of them had sprained a wrist and ended up in hospital.

But they'd not once actually discussed like ... whether they were *dating*, or not.

Eloise didn't even know if he wanted a relationship.

She didn't even know if *she* wanted a relationship.

She'd thought she was pretty much over Josh until Christmas began creeping closer, and she'd realised how weird it would be this year without him. Maybe not *worse*, but ... different. And it played on her mind more and more with her parents going away and Cara not planning to be around much.

It was probably less about Josh and more about her, but so what?

Grabbing up the cutlery and dropping it into the washing-up bowl, she changed the subject. "What time are you getting to mine then, on Wednesday?"

"Wednesday?"

"Christmas."

"Oh, right, sorry. Er ... eleven? I guess?"

"Right. I'm thinking dinner at half twelve. Is George coming? Did you ask him?"

"He says he's going back to his parents for Christmas now, since his sister's home, and his mum's staying with them too. And what about your Jamie?"

"He's not *my* Jamie. And he's going home for Christmas too. So it's just us. A guy-free Christmas."

"Except for Santa."

"Except for Santa," she conceded, smiling. Cara seemed to have found the Christmas spirit at last. "Did you see the big sacks of presents in the living room for us? I only asked them for a couple of movies on iTunes and some Spotify vouchers."

"I know! I think my Christmas list had like, four things on it. And one of those was that nice Clinique face cream I like."

"I bet they've got you thermals," Eloise guessed, pouring the washing-up water away now it was done. "You're always complaining how cold your room is. And socks. I bet they've got us loads of socks. Like we don't have enough."

"To be fair, I really need some new socks."

"Me too."

They caught each other's eye again and giggled.

It was good to have her sister around.

Eloise hugged her parents in turn, kissing them goodbye.

"Are you sure you've got everything, now?" she asked them.

"Aren't we the ones who should be asking her that?" her dad muttered to her mum, loudly, and Eloise laughed sarcastically. "We'll be fine, kiddo. Almost all packed."

"I left you a Post-it on the bathroom mirror so you don't forget your toothbrushes. And text me when you get to the airport, and when you board, and when you land, and –"

Her mum kissed her again on the cheek. "And when we get to the hotel. And *you* text when you get home safe. Drive carefully. It's gotten icy."

"They're saying it might snow," her dad said.

"It won't snow," Eloise scoffed. Christmas was already all wrong this year, and the last thing that would happen was a white Christmas. A frosty one, at best.

(But if it did snow, maybe her parents' flight would be cancelled, and they wouldn't go away on holiday, and Christmas would be back to normal.)

Eloise crossed her fingers behind her back for a moment. "And you've got all the presents, now?"

"Yes, all in the car."

Also in the car – Cara, who was beeping the horn. Eloise gave her the finger over her shoulder. They had half an hour to make the ten-minute drive to the station for Cara's train.

"And the food?"

Clearly, Eloise took after her mum in some way. While Cara and their mum seemed to share the same sort of pressurised work ethic, Eloise and her mum were both worriers. Her friends had given her the nickname 'Mama Hen' in their group chat at uni after that time she'd taken tissues and plasters on a night out.

"Yup. Thanks again." They'd bought her a tub of Heroes,

140

some of the nice Marks and Spencer's biscuits they always had, a tin of shortbread exactly like the one already in her cupboard she was keeping for Christmas, a bottle of Bucks Fizz and a dozen mince pies. Eloise already had it all at home, but didn't want to seem ungrateful or upset them. She'd just take them into school after the holidays. Jamie would probably scoff all the mince pies, if she offered him them. And she could send Cara back with whatever leftovers she could carry.

Cara pressed on the horn again, longer this time.

"Right. Her Ladyship is calling. I'll see you both when you get back."

She gave them a last hug before dashing off to the car with the bag of food, her dad having already loaded her car up with the presents.

Her phone pinged with a text as she climbed into the car, and she barely got it out of the back pocket of her jeans before Cara snatched it out of her hands.

"Ah-ah, no driving and texting. Come on. I can't miss this train. Ooh, it's a text from Jamie. He wants to know what time you'll be home. Winky face. Ew. Do people still send winky faces when they're not like, ironic?"

"What's wrong with a winky face?"

Eloise looked over long enough for Cara to do an over-exaggerated wink, making her snort with laughter.

"Shall I tell him that you've decided to remain abstinent until marriage?"

"You can, but then I could go on George's Facebook

from your account and like some random old photos from
six years ago."

"Truce?"

"'Tis the season," Eloise agreed, and turned up the
volume on her Christmas mix CD as she turned out of
the street.

Three days until Christmas

Chapter 13

"Y̶ou know it's supposed to snow," Jamilla commented, looking at the bleak view out of the kitchen window. Bleak because their house backed onto a narrow alley between their street and the next, and bleak because, even though it was one in the afternoon, it was grey and drizzling.

"It won't snow," Henry and Cara said at the same time. Cara went on, "It's rainy out, anyway. Even if it did snow – and in London – it'll never settle."

"And besides," said Henry, "when was the last time we had a white Christmas?"

"We had some snow on Boxing Day a couple of years ago," Jamilla said.

"And in early December when I was like, thirteen," Cara added.

"Yeah, but still. You know what I mean. We never get snow for the twenty-fifth, and snow hardly ever happens in London. And just as well – they'd cancel my train at the first sight of a snowflake. And I don't know about you two, but I can't wait to get home for Christmas. Have a proper home-cooked meal."

"Oi! What do you call this?" Cara gestured with the spoon at the pan she was busy stirring on the stove. "This is Jamie's finest risotto."

"I'm still not convinced." Henry looked at it warily.

"Please! When has dear Mr Oliver ever steered us wrong?" Jamilla cried, finally pulling herself away from the window to carry on chopping mushrooms. Cara had been relegated to stirring the risotto continuously while the other two took care of the actual cooking. Although, right now, Henry was busy pulling leftover crackers by himself, and was wearing three crinkly party hats and not doing much cooking.

With their other two housemates gone for the holidays already, and Jamilla getting her flight back to Glasgow later that evening, they were having a mock-up Christmas meal with the three of them before Christmas. They had crackers, cheap white wine and ... risotto.

Although, to be fair, Henry had prepared a cinnamon apple crumble, which smelled delightfully Christmassy every time one of them opened the fridge.

This weekend was the first time since – well, since last year, at best – that Cara had really felt festive. Really been

144

excited for Christmas. After she'd heard the truth from George and hadn't had to break up with him she'd been on such a high she'd got a last-minute bus back home to see her parents before their holiday, and she'd spent the morning wrapping presents. She'd even impulse-purchased some bows to stick on them when she'd been out buying the bottles of wine for dinner.

Eloise would love the bows. And she couldn't deny that they did look that bit nicer.

Even if the wrapping paper had been three rolls for a quid, and ripped a few too many times.

She'd show her sister. She was no Scrooge or Grinch or even a Harry or Marv. She could do Christmas *and* work hard.

Jamilla sang along to *Blue Christmas*, pouring in some more stock as Cara kept stirring. Henry made them both jump, pulling another cracker.

"Who's Santa's favourite singer?"

"Who?"

"*Elfis.*" He wheezed. "I love that one. Elfis. Classic."

Jamilla and Cara exchanged a look long enough to roll their eyes at him. There was a reason that he'd had a book of Christmas cracker jokes in their house Secret Santa.

There was probably a reason Cara had had a stress ball and a black Santa hat that said 'Bah Humbug'.

She was being a good sport about it though: she was wearing it now while they cooked.

"When are you seeing Pudding and Pie to exchange gifts, then?" Henry asked her.

"Who and who?"

"Georgie Porgie. Like the nursery rhyme. Also known as the good friend you so callously stole from me."

"Ignore him," Jamilla sighed, sweeping the mushrooms into the pan after poking the risotto with a fork. "He's been drinking beer since he woke up at ten."

With a cry of outrage, Henry launched half of a pulled cracker at her head, making them all laugh. "I had one!"

"And you had it before twelve."

"Uh, it's *Christmas*. Time for eating all day long and drinking all day too?"

"Well, keep it up and you'll be rolling through that doorway when you're back in January." Jamilla leant over the stove, nibbling a bit of risotto from her fork. "Mm. Almost done. Five minutes more and we're good to go. I'll grate the cheese ready. Henry, can you grab some plates? Pour the wine?"

"Yes, chef!"

And five minutes later they all had plates full of warm baguette and risotto, Christmas crackers piled on the footstool in front of them, the three of them squished onto one sofa, wine glasses full near their feet and *Home Alone* on the TV.

"Alright," Henry sighed contentedly. "*Now* it's Christmas."

Cara and Henry stayed downstairs the rest of the afternoon, watching whatever crap was on TV, sharing a packet of supermarket-brand value custard creams in lieu of any fancier biscuits. Cara had her laptop, doing some work, and Henry was reading on his Kindle.

Jamilla huffed as she hauled her suitcase down the stairs.

"Do you want a hand?" Henry yelled.

"I've got it," she panted back, and the two of them stifled giggles as she puffed and struggled downstairs for the next five minutes. "Phew! Right, you two nerds, I'm off. Merry Christmas and all that jazz! See you in the New Year!"

Cara brushed some crumbs off her lap, setting down her laptop as she got up. Jamilla hugged her and Henry in turn as they said their goodbyes, wished each other safe trips home and happy Christmases.

"Got enough?"

"It's mostly presents," she defended herself, looking at her massive suitcase and stuffed carry-on bag.

It was only when Jamilla opened the door that they all fell silent.

Henry broke it with a gasp, shoving past the girls and stepping out onto the step barefoot. It must've been freezing: the steps were stone, and damp. He craned his head back, mouth open. "Well, fuck me. Snow."

"Oh, God," Jamilla groaned. "Bollocks. This better not stick."

"It's sticking to the gatepost," Cara pointed out, feeling sick at the sight of it. Snow was the last thing she wanted – or needed – this week. Everything came to a standstill and once one car or person had disturbed it, it looked crap too. It just got in the way.

She squeezed Jamilla's arm, giving her an encouraging smile. The poor girl's face was crestfallen. "I'm sure your flight will be fine. You said Glasgow Airport was still running fine, and the snow stopped there this afternoon. I'm sure it'll be fine."

Because it would be.

This was *London*. London was tougher than a little snow that was barely settling and would probably turn to sleet and rain in less than an hour. The airports wouldn't stop for this. Neither would the trains, or the Tube, or the buses, or the taxis.

And besides – they'd been forecast snow all day, and this was the first they were seeing of it.

It wouldn't come to anything.

Jamilla was home five hours later, face red and puffy and furious, and she'd quite obviously been crying.

Cara had been back and forth to the window every half hour to look at the snow. It had turned into a blizzard about an hour after Jamilla had left and hadn't stopped. They'd turned the TV over to the news channel, where at least eighty per cent of the stories had been about the sudden weather disruption.

Airports were closing or, at the very least, flights were being delayed. A couple of non-fatal car accidents on major motorways. Train services had stopped in many parts of the country. Roads had been closed in some places.

Travellers were being warned to be extremely cautious,

and the local news said not to travel unless absolutely necessary.

Cara was pretty sure that everyone here considered their travel necessary, whatever it was for. Actually – all over the country. She knew her mum would've dragged her dad out for milk in this weather, just to make sure they had plenty in case they were snowed in for the next few days.

Oh, God.

"What if we're snowed in for the next few days?" she'd asked Henry in a wild moment of panic at one point. "We've run all the food down because we're all going away for the holidays."

"Don't be such a drama queen," he'd told her, but turned a worried face back onto his phone, where he was looking up alternate routes home.

And then Jamilla was storming in, on the verge of breaking down into tears (again) and kicking her suitcase into the hallway. "I hate airports. I hate aeroplanes. I hate snow. I hate Christmas."

"What did they say?" Henry asked, dithering in the doorway.

"Oh!" She stormed into the living room, throwing herself down in the middle of the other sofa. "They can offer me a full refund! Or get me on the next flight out!"

"When's that?"

"There's a few due to be going out tomorrow but what good is that if it's still snowed over? I put my name on the list, but I just know it won't be going out. I can *feel* it."

"I'll put the kettle on," Cara said quietly, extracting herself from the sofa again. She was glad she'd thought to buy some milk with a longer date on it so there would be milk for her when she got back on Boxing Day. At least they'd have plenty for the next few days, if the three of them were stuck here.

When she got back, Jamilla was sniffling, watching the news with big, blank eyes. She took one of the mugs from the tray Cara was carrying.

"Well, if you can't fly out, at least they'll give you a refund."

Jamilla burst into tears.

"Nice going, Scrooge," Henry muttered, and moved across to give their sobbing housemate a cuddle and placate her with better sentiments.

She was a rubbish, rubbish sort of person.

"What's the weather like by you?"

It was almost midnight, but Eloise was still awake – apparently, Cara had caught her with perfect timing: in the ad break of *Die Hard*.

"Oh, just a dusting! It's fine, really. They've salted the roads and stuff. It's mostly just sticking on the grass and the tops of the cars, but the roads are pretty clear. We're off out to the pub in a bit."

"Be alright getting snowed in there," Cara joked, her voice uneven. "Plenty of food and drink and festive cheer to keep you happy."

Eloise laughed. "Fingers crossed, huh? What about you? I saw your Snapchats. And I saw on my news app that the snow was really bad in London. Makes a change, doesn't it?"

"Jamilla's flight home was cancelled. They're not sure if the trains will still be running tomorrow."

"Well –" Eloise sighed, and plastered on a wide smile, "– it's got to thaw, hasn't it? And it's only the twenty-second. There's still a couple of days to go. It'll be fine. I'm sure it'll be fine. Is your bus still running?"

"They've not cancelled it yet. They've not cancelled anything past tonight, yet. But it's not looking good. Look, El, I'm just worried if ... well ... I mean ..."

"No. No, don't even say it. Don't even *think* it, Cara. You'll jinx it. There's still a few days to Christmas and for the snow to stop and the roads to clear and everything – *everything* – is going to be fine."

Two days till Christmas

Chapter 14

Jamie stood at the window with his hands on his hips. "I think I've made a horrible mistake."

Eloise set down their hot chocolates. "Which is?"

"Not taking today and tomorrow off work."

"Because ...?"

He could hardly complain of actually having to work – he'd been sent home at lunchtime when the snow didn't let up, and they'd said unless it melted overnight, the office would be closed the next day too.

She was glad it hadn't snowed like this last week, when she'd been in work. Chances were, she'd have been there before they decided to shut the school, and it would *not* have been a nice drive home. Jamie said it had taken him almost half an hour longer than usual – and he'd not even been able to get his car up the hill to the flats. Like many other drivers, he'd had to leave it on the side of the main road.

Her old Polo never would've made it.

"Because then I'd have driven home during the weekend."

Eloise went back to the kitchen for the biscuits. "I'm sure it'll thaw. They've not even forecast any more snow. It's supposed to stop in the next hour or so."

Jamie tore himself away from the window, plonking down on the sofa so close their legs were pressed together. Eloise swung hers onto his lap, wondering how this felt so comfortable – so *normal* – so suddenly.

"Some of the trains are still running," she ventured. "And a few buses. And it might still melt."

"Mm."

This was the neighbour she thought she knew: withdrawn and sullen and not-too-talkative. Arsey. But she reached out to squeeze his knee.

"It'll be okay," she murmured.

"Do you think it's something you grow out of? Not listening to your mum? She kept telling me I should've gone home this weekend and I kept saying it'd be fine and she was only bloody right, wasn't she?"

"Well, my mum's all but skipping Christmas, and if I listened to her, I'd be having a seafood buffet for tea and staying in a sea-view room on the fifth floor, where the walls are thin enough that I can hear the couple on the floor above having sex and the family next door yelling because someone forgot to pack towels."

"Sounds ... delightful." He turned to her, head twisting so he could squint at her. "Do you think the walls are thin enough here that Number One and Number Two can hear us having sex?"

Eloise felt her cheeks catch fire. She hadn't even thought about that. It hadn't even crossed her mind. She could hear Number Six, above her, when she wore high heels, and when she hoovered.

"Probably not," she hoped out loud.

Jamie laughed, stretching his neck out a little more to peck her on the jaw. "Don't look so mortified. I'm only teasing."

She swatted his arm, shoving him away with a pout before letting her face fall back, giggling. She pushed him back upright to pick up her hot chocolate. Jamie sighed, moving to pick up his mug too.

His eyes fixed on the window for another while longer.

"Hey," Eloise said, "worst come to worst, you'll be stuck here for Christmas, with my amazing turkey and beautiful roast potatoes and Sainsbury's best Christmas pudding that I'll try to light on fire and probably fail at, and all the crap TV you could wish for."

"You're really selling this, you know. But you realise if we're snowed in, it's probably just the two of us. Cara probably won't be able to get here."

She knew.

She was just trying really, really hard not to think about that.

"What do you do for Christmas? With your family? Tell me all about it."

So he did. How they all opened their stockings and drank hot chocolate. Then they'd all have to get dressed, and his dad would make poached egg on toast for breakfast, and then they'd wait for grandparents and an uncle and cousin to arrive while they all pitched in to cook the dinner before they could open any other presents. Christmas dinner at one o'clock exactly, followed by trifle and a Christmas pudding only his granddad ever ate, and they'd watch all the Christmas specials on the telly, play board games, and it was leftover turkey sandwiches for tea.

It wasn't like Eloise's Christmas, but it sounded glorious.

Then he wanted to hear about hers, so she told him.

They'd all be awake by seven, eating bacon sandwiches around the tree, all the presents torn open by ten (and only when they paced themselves). They'd all get dressed up in ugly Christmas jumpers, go for a walk before lunch and play trivia games all afternoon. Her dad would fall asleep on the sofa, but wake up in time for the *Doctor Who* special. They'd argue over what new releases to watch on the movie channels, getting tipsy and giggly and eating themselves into food comas with spring rolls and pork pies and bags of crisps that would keep them up until past midnight.

"You don't cook on Christmas Day?" he asked, when she hadn't mentioned it.

Eloise snorted. "So we used to, but one year when I was like, eleven, my dad had a complete meltdown over it. Nothing was going right. The cheese sauce for the cauliflower cheese curdled, the roasties weren't cooked properly, he forgot all about the stuffing, and then burned the turkey. It was *chaos*. So now we cook on Christmas Eve, just in case of future disasters like the Great Turkeypocalypse. It was just as well we had all the crisps and spring rolls and stuff in."

"Well," Jamie said then, "I'm glad you're not a leftovers-for-tea sort of family, because if we do get snowed in, at least I know you've got enough food to see us through till March."

"Oh, ha-ha, laugh it up. And I know you stole that box of mince pies from me. I saw it in your recycling bin."

"How do you know I didn't buy them myself?"

"Because I know you don't shop at Aldi."

"Maybe I went there just for the mince pies."

"Likely story."

He lifted her hand towards him, kissing the inside of her wrist. Her hand dropped over his shoulder, their fingers still locked together at the tips. He was warm and smelled of spice and Eloise caught herself with that stupid goofy smile on her face again as she looked at him.

The snow was still falling outside.

One day till Christmas

Chapter 15

The snow had been cleared enough for Jamilla to get a flight to Scotland.

And the trains had been running yesterday – limited services, with delays and disruption, but Henry had managed to get home. Everything would be fine tomorrow. The snow was already starting to disappear. It'd be gone by the next morning, she was sure.

She'd managed to get into the office, slipping around on the ice on the walk between her house and the Tube stop, and the Tube stop and the office. Only a few of them were still working on Christmas Eve, with only half of *them* making it to the office.

The snow had stopped after the blizzard-like incident on Sunday evening, but the whole city was disrupted by the inches of slush and the ice that covered almost every pavement and half the roads.

It wasn't snowing, but it was still bloody freezing. And the office's radiators had chosen today to not work properly.

"Pipes are frozen, or something. It's affected the whole building, I asked reception," Marcus announced to everyone, having gone downstairs about ten o'clock. "But – the good news is, I'm heading out on a coffee run. Someone come give me a hand. I can't carry seven coffees and open all those doors on my own."

Freddie, one of their social media gurus, stood up. "I volunteer!"

"Alright, Katniss, get your coat on," Marcus laughed. "Everyone text me your orders, or else you're all getting lattes of the festive variety. I'll never remember them all otherwise."

Someone was blasting out a Christmas album from the other side of the office. Tinsel had been strung up everywhere – more had appeared since last week, as if the days left until Christmas and the amount of tinsel were inversely proportional. There was a box of Celebrations and some more mince pies in the kitchenette area, already half-gone.

And nobody – *nobody* – seemed to be working.

Cara glanced up, the chatter loud and grating on her. Everyone else had their laptops open, computers on, emails open, but they were all talking across the office to each other, voices rising with building excitement the more they all talked about their plans for the next few days.

If they weren't going to work, why did they bother coming in at all?

She had so much to get done – especially if she was taking the next two days off, and then the weekend ... She had articles to finish editing and proof-read before they scheduled them, and content that needed drafting that she wanted to get a head start on, and the book club still needed refining ...

"What about you, Cara?"

"Huh?" She didn't lift her head from the screen. Emails were still pouring into her inbox. Who was even working? It was Christmas. Shouldn't they all be home with their families, or something? Why were they getting back to her now, of all days, with outlines of sponsored articles or feedback on ones she'd sent back to them? Didn't they know how much she had to do today?

"When are you going home to the fam?"

"Er, tomorrow. Getting the bus to my sister's."

"Tomorrow? A *bus*?"

She wrote 'tomorrow' in the email she was sending and huffed, scowling at herself before amending it.

Jen, she noticed, did a great job of jumping into the conversation and distracting the rest of the office from Cara's plans, and she looked up long enough to shoot Jen a quick smile and quiet, "Thank you."

Then Marcus and Freddie returned with the coffees, singing a carol, and Cara began to lose all hope of getting anything done in the next few hours before Marcus shooed them all home early so they could get back to their families.

She had better things to do than get back to an empty house. She had so much work to do.

Two-thirty rolled around before she even noticed, and Jen shook the back of her chair. "Come on, turn that thing off. It's time to go home! It's Christmas!"

"One sec," she muttered. "I just need to finish ... this bit here ..."

Jen spun her chair away and someone else swooped in, grabbing up her laptop as she shrieked in horror. It was Becky from Graphics, and Cara protested when she clicked at the laptop and shut it.

"Don't worry, it's all saved, it's not going anywhere."

"That's what I'm worried about."

"Cara." Jen perched on her desk. "What's the earliest deadline any of that has to be up?"

"The ninth."

"And when are you back in work?"

"Friday."

"So you've got what, two weeks to sort it?"

"But –"

Jen reached behind her for the laptop, handing it to Becky, who put it into Cara's rucksack for her. "There. Work is finished for Christmas. And I don't want to hear you've been online before Friday. You leave that thing at home when you go to your sister's, do you hear?"

Cara forced out a laugh, even though she was itching

to pull the laptop back out and finish the piece she'd been editing. There were only a few hundred words left to go. And only two other pieces she wanted to do final edits on. And –

"I don't think she'll do it," Jen said.

"Me either."

"Don't think who will do what?" Freddie asked, walking over, already bundled up against the cold in touch screen-friendly gloves and earmuffs, bag hanging from one shoulder.

"Cara. Stop working over Christmas."

"Pfft. Never. The girl's a machine." He grinned at her. "She'd run this place single-handedly if we asked her to."

The way they all seemed to say that about her made her wonder if it was such a bad reputation.

"I'm just doing my job," she murmured. Was it that bad? What was so wrong with having a strong work ethic?

"There's working hard, and then there's working yourself to the bone and not leaving time for anything else. Sweetie, you've just got to have a balance," Jen said gently.

"How about, like most of the rest of us, you leave your laptop and stuff here?" Freddie added.

"Because –"

"Marcus!" Becky yelled, seeing him leaving his office. "Marcus, back us up, here. Tell Cara to leave her laptop here over Christmas. She'll have to listen to you."

"But I –"

"No ifs, no buts, no roasting chestnuts," Marcus said,

raising his hands. "I'm with the rest of the guys on this one, Cara. You need a break. Otherwise you'll be no good to us."

"You've been burning that midnight oil too long," Jen said, and reached to poke under her eyes gently. "Look at those bags. They'd class as hold luggage."

"Piss off," Cara laughed, but it didn't feel funny.

"Work can wait till the New Year," Marcus told her. "Rest up, properly, and come back ready to tackle everything. We want you on top form if you're going to be taking on Dave's role. Now, shut that thing in the drawer and come on. I need to get this place locked up and you lot are holding me up."

Now that, coming from her boss – and with the comment about the promotion – was enough to kick Cara into gear, packing her rucksack up, but not before Jen peeled her laptop out of it and put it in her desk drawer with her collection of breakfast bars, tea bags and note-books. She whined (actually whined, to her shame), but left it behind all the same.

(It wasn't like she didn't get her emails on her phone, after all.)

The five of them piled out onto the icy streets, where Freddie promptly slipped and went flying straight into a lamppost, throwing his arms around it to stay upright.

Jen giggled. "It's like in *Muppet Christmas Carol*! When Kermit leaves work on Christmas Eve and does the ice skating!"

164

They all laughed, Cara knowing Eloise would've said exactly the same thing. Freddie stuck one foot out hesitantly, finding a better patch of pavement to lunge towards. Marcus and Becky were going in the other direction, so they all said their goodbyes and wished each other a Happy Christmas, before starting home.

"I can't believe you humiliated me like that," she muttered to Jen, once they were on the Tube, Freddie having got a train in the other direction.

"You needed a good kick up the arse," Jen told her, sticking her chin out. "It's not good for you."

"I'm fine! There's nothing wrong with me. Unless it's suddenly a crime to love your job."

"Yeah, right now you are, but carry on like you've been going and you'll put yourself in hospital in six years. You'll end up having to retire at thirty. Move to the seaside where the fresh air will restore you, and have your sister move in and spoon-feed you beef broth and knit you blankets to keep the chill away."

"You've been reading *Little Women* again, haven't you?"

Jen rolled her eyes but didn't deny it. "I'm serious. Everyone's saying it, you know, not just me. That you work too hard and you'll make yourself ill. Even Marcus."

"Do you all gossip about me behind my back?"

"It's not gossip! We just worry about you. They had to force you to take your holiday days, Cara. That's not normal."

She bit her lip.

When you put it like that ... maybe Jen had a little bit of a point. Just a *little* bit.

They didn't talk the rest of the journey, but both had to get off at the same stop to switch lines. They stopped in a quiet section, out the way of the tunnels and escalators.

"I didn't mean to upset you," Jen said.

"You didn't. Promise." Cara smiled to prove it. "Just ... shifted my perspective, a little. Anyway. Don't run off yet – I forgot to give you your present."

Jen laughed. "Oh, good. Much as I love giving, I think I like receiving a little more."

They both fished into their bags, Cara pulling out a Lush gift set she'd wrapped up for Jen, complete with a slightly-squashed bow. Jen was always posting on Instagram with whatever bath bomb she was trying out, so Cara knew she'd like the gift.

Her own package was misshapen and bulky, squishy in some places and hard in others.

"What the bloody hell –?"

Jen shook her own package, and looked her dead in the eye. "I bet it's a dog."

Cara lifted hers. "I bet it's a book."

"Oh, I'm going to miss you! I know I'll text you, but – I'll miss you!" Jen hugged her tight and Cara laughed, hugging her back. "Merry Christmas, sweetie!"

"You too. Safe travels tonight!"

"And you, in the morning!"

They shoved their presents into their bags and hugged once more before dashing off for their rides home. Cara was relieved she managed to nab a seat for the rest of the journey, hugging her bag on her lap and people-watching.

There were harried-looking people in suits, frowning at their phones, still working.

There were giggling groups, decked out in tinsel and reindeer headbands.

There were people in Santa hats and in Christmas jumpers, flushed and a little bored-looking, just wanting to *get* there, already, wherever *there* was.

There were sleepy couples and families, leaning on each other, talking quietly.

There were the flustered last-minute shoppers, looking completely knackered and mostly relieved, carrier bags and totes shoved between their legs.

Cara looked at all of them, drinking it all in, wondering which category she fell into. She knew she'd be working, if she had her laptop. She knew Eloise would be giddy, even if she weren't drunk.

And she knew if George were here, they'd be one of the soppy, sweet-looking couples holding hands, heads together, just looking at each other, and happy.

Eight hours till Christmas

Chapter 16

Eloise was having flashbacks to a few weeks ago, when Cara had called her to say that she wouldn't be coming home until the afternoon of Christmas Day.

Because right now, it was four o'clock on Christmas Eve, and she had the turkey in the oven, and the sprouts and cauliflower and broccoli were all boiling away, and – and Cara, bloody Cara, was saying she might not bother coming up tomorrow.

"I don't understand," Eloise said, turning the knobs on the oven down a little and moving into the living room. "Say that again."

"I'm just not sure." Cara would be biting her lip now, maybe fidgeting with her hair. "What with all the ice on the roads, and the snow's still hanging around. And they've forecast more, you know? It's already snowing back home."

"And? So what, you might get snowed in here. Is that the end of the world?"

Cara hesitated, long enough that she made it clear how she felt about it.

Eloise let out a harsh, hollow bark of laughter. "I see."

"Oh, come on, don't be like that. They've already said they might cancel my bus if the roads get too dangerous. And there's nothing going tonight I can get a ticket for. Everything that's going is full."

"The trains are running."

"Well, yes, but ... Well, it might be fine tomorrow. I mean, it probably will be. I'm just saying, if it isn't ..."

But the cost of a train ticket wasn't worth it. Not for Christmas. Not to see her twin sister.

"You know what, Cara? It's fine. Don't bother. Who fucking needs Christmas anyway? What do I care?"

"I'll come up in a couple of days. The next chance I get to come up. I'll stay for New Year's instead. We can do a late Christmas."

"I've already got the turkey cooking!"

"Why? I wasn't going to be there till lunchtime tomorrow anyway. How bloody big is the turkey?"

"I thought I'd do it today so there's no fuss tomorrow, like Dad always does, and it can be ready for whenever you get here, even if you're late. But it's fine. Stay in London. Get all the work done you want in that big, bleak house all on your own, and skip Christmas. God knows, everybody else is." She was about to hang up when Cara barrelled on.

"That's not fair, Eloise. I'm just trying to be sensible about it. It's not that I don't want to come —"

"Don't give me that bullshit!" she barked down the phone. "We all know you didn't really want to come visit for Christmas. You're too wrapped up in your bloody job. You barely even make time for your boyfriend, never mind your *sister*."

"I do so make time for him! And you! You're the one with no social life, who stays cooped up in her flat every evening, or going home to Mum and Dad practically every other weekend. That's not my fault."

Eloise scoffed. As if that was *her* fault. "We can't all be good at making a new best friend everywhere we go."

"I don't do that. And you have plenty of friends."

"No, I have plenty of *your* friends. Just like always. They're only my friend because I tagged along with you all the time."

"You're being ridiculous."

She wasn't exactly sure how they'd gotten so far away from Cara's jeopardised travel plans, but right now Eloise was finding it really hard to let this go. She'd opened the floodgates and there was no turning back now.

"No, I'm not. This is how it's always been. Which is fine. But don't have a go at me because I'm not as extroverted as you, and act like it's my fault I'll be spending

Christmas alone because *you* can't be bothered to make it happen, and because *you* think your job is so bloody important. Do you think the rest of us don't care about our jobs?"

"You've got to be fucking kidding me," Cara muttered. Eloise heard her sister's temper rising then as her voice got louder and sharper. "Some of us actually have to work hard to make things happen, El. Some of us actually have to put the effort in. It doesn't all fall nicely into place for some of us."

"Since when has everything just *fallen into place* for me?"

"Since always! You never had to work hard at school. I was the one who had to keep up with you. And you've always acted like you're the one that's so hard done by."

She didn't do that. Did she? She didn't do that.

"Well, maybe I wouldn't if you didn't act like such a martyr. Nobody's making you work so hard."

"Everyone had to rally around you when Josh ran off with another girl, but maybe he wouldn't have done if you weren't such an ungrateful bitch sometimes."

Eloise staggered back, blinking, her mouth hanging open. Had Cara actually just said that? Grinding her teeth, Eloise gripped the phone so tight her knuckles turned white.

"Well, forgive me for trying to salvage Christmas after you ruined it."

"I don't get why it's such a big deal! We'll all get together anyway soon. It's not like I booked Mum and Dad on that holiday. And it's not like it's my fault you're being so whiny over not having Josh around, even when you have a perfectly good guy right across the hall."

"Did you ever stop to think I go and see Mum and Dad so much because I'm homesick, and I hate being alone like this, and I miss you? Did you even *consider* how shitty you'd make me feel by not caring enough to come home for Christmas?"

"El ..."

"Have a Merry fucking Christmas in London, Cara."

She hung up before Cara could try to defend herself, and burst into tears.

Her sister was a horrible, horrible person who'd ruined Christmas.

Eloise cried it out for a while, snotty and loud, sitting on the kitchen floor, back against the radiator and watching the turkey cook in the oven, until the timer went off. Sniffing hard, Eloise rubbed her hands over her face, wiped her nose on a tissue from her apron pocket. She clambered to her feet and went to the bathroom to splash cold water on her face.

She looked like she'd been crying. Eyes red and swollen. Nose red on the end like Rudolph. Cheeks a bit blotchy.

But she also looked ready for a Christmas that wasn't happening any more. The sleeves of her Christmas jumper were scrunched up around her elbows, an apron tied around her waist and dusted with water and butter. She'd pulled her hair back into a bun on top of her head, but it had since fallen loose, hung halfway to the nape of her neck, strands flying out everywhere. The burn on the back of her forearm she'd got an hour ago was still red and angry, so she slapped a little Savlon on it. Savlon would cure everything that a good cup of tea couldn't, she was convinced.

Except Christmas.

Nothing could fix this Christmas.

The thought made her eyes water again, but a knock at the door startled her before she started crying again. Eloise wiped her hands over her face again, like she could wipe away the redness, and gave up promptly to answer the door.

It was probably Jamie. He'd said he'd stop by before he left, to say goodbye.

She hoped his kind of goodbye didn't involve having sex – she had a Christmas dinner to prepare.

(Even if nobody would be around to eat it.)

And she looked and felt like crap.

Jamie's face looked funny when she opened the door, she thought. Harried. Moody. He looked every inch the arsey, brooding neighbour she knew so well.

Whatever it was disappeared quickly as he blinked at her, concern replacing his previous expression. "Have you been crying?"

"Onions," she lied. She didn't want to delay him getting home by spilling the story, or pushing her sadness onto him when he'd be home and having a nice Christmas with his family in about two hours.

He didn't look convinced.

"Are you all ready to go?" she asked, stepping back, not sure if he was going to come in or not. He didn't have his coat or shoes on – was still wearing his slippers, actually. His hair stuck up on end at the front, like he'd been tugging at it.

"I *was*. Dad's just rung. The snow's really bad by them. I didn't even think to check. I just made sure my car wasn't snowed in here and the motorways were still open. They've been calling for hours and I didn't even notice. I keep forgetting I turned the vibrate off when my phone's on silent."

"Why would you even do that? Who does that? You'll miss all your messages."

"Clearly. I'm an idiot. I've ruined Christmas."

"Wait – what do you mean? Ruined Christmas?"

He couldn't have ruined it worse than Cara, surely.

"The roads are really bad back home. Mum doesn't want me driving in it. She's worried I'll get stranded somewhere, or break down, or crash. I can't even get a bus because there's no buses running. I can get to the next town, if I'm lucky. And walk the next two hours. Probably take me longer, actually, in the snow."

"God," Eloise breathed, her own Christmas chaos forgotten. "What are you going to do?"

He shrugged. "Wait it out. It's meant to stop in the next

few hours and, with any luck, people will venture out then and clear some of the roads, so I can get back. Might have to drive back tomorrow. Otherwise, I might be scrounging some turkey dinner off you." He punctuated it with a smirk, but his eyes were uneasy. He wanted to get home. Eloise couldn't blame him.

"Well, there'll be plenty to go around," she said, forcing herself to sound upbeat, leaving him to follow as she went back to the kitchen. "Cara's not coming."

"Eh?"

"Yup. Not coming. They've cancelled her bus because of the ice, and she won't get a train. She said she'd come for New Year instead. Which means we'll both be spending tomorrow on our own. Except, like, together. How's that for a new relationship? Not even decided if we're official yet and spending Christmas together."

Jaime was quiet for a moment, long enough that she glanced back over at him. He gave an awkward smile, rubbing his cheek. "Am I meant to just ignore that comment about the state of our relationship?"

"I didn't mean it like that."

"Yeah, I know. But, I mean, since you brought it up ..." Jamie pulled her away from the oven, holding her hands and getting down on one knee. "Eloise, would you like to be my actual, proper girlfriend?"

"Don't be so daft," she told him, rolling her eyes and tugging him back up. But her insides had turned to goo in that way they did when he smiled like that, and she kissed his cheek. "Alright, then. Since you asked so nicely."

"My mum said I should bring you home for Christmas, you know," he added, opening the fridge and searching for something he'd be allowed to snack on. He said it so nonchalantly that Eloise took a moment to realise what he'd just said.

"Did she?"

Jamie shrugged, giving up his search and closing the fridge. "I mean, you were supposed to be spending Christmas with Cara, which is why I didn't bring it up. But if she can't make it and I go back home, you can come with me. If you like."

Eloise smiled, but it faltered quickly. "That's a really nice offer, don't get me wrong; it's just ..."

"You wanted to spend it with your sister. No, I get it. Aren't there any trains?"

"She might have to spend more than ten quid on a train," Eloise muttered, stabbing a carrot rather viciously as she checked on them. Almost done, at least. She'd have to get the potatoes on soon. Better start peeling them.

"So ... why are you still cooking Christmas dinner?"

"I wish I knew."

Because she didn't know what else to do, frankly.

And *she* bloody well wasn't missing out on her Christmas dinner. Even if she might be eating it for the next week to get through the leftovers. Although now it looked like she might end up spending it with Jamie and his family. Which wouldn't be so bad; actually, it was very sweet, since he'd obviously talked a lot about her for his mum to suggest bringing her home for the holidays. It was just ... not the way she'd pictured it being. Not how it should be, this year. Not with Cara spending Christmas alone.

"I just can't believe this." Jamie sighed, walking towards the kettle. He lifted it slightly, eyebrows raised, asking for permission. Eloise nodded. Tea definitely wouldn't go amiss right now.

Or some Baileys, since it was Christmas.

"I mean, all the years we never get any snow until March, and now there's about eight years' worth of it in a week, and right at Christmas. Sod a white Christmas. Why can't it hold off until January, at least? When I've not got time off already, and the office has to shut and give me *extra* time off."

"But you love your job."

"Doesn't mean I don't love a good lazy day with my Amazon Prime too. Speaking of ..."

"Yes, yes, you can go put something on the telly. Just not *Outlander*." They'd started watching it the other night. "I'll be in and out cooking for the next few hours and I'm not missing any of that."

It was weird how domestic that sounded coming out of her mouth, with a guy she'd barely spoken to only last month.

A guy who was now her *boyfriend*.

Despite everything that was going wrong, the thought did make her heart swell.

"Are you vetoing any Christmas films? I was gonna watch *Arthur Christmas*. I love that one."

"Ooh, yes! Yeah, stick that on." She could handle missing bits of that one; she'd seen it enough times.

"Am I allowed to have any of your fancy biscuits yet?"

"It's not Christmas!"

He started to say something, but stopped himself. It might've been that she was being stupid, or it might've been that it wasn't like Cara would care, but either way, he didn't say any of that. Just –

"Roger that, chef. Biscuits are off-limits. Oh – or did you want a hand cooking? Sorry. I probably should've offered that first. I'm going to be blacklisted from your long list of Christmas dinner invitees at this rate."

"Nope. I've got this all under control."

Cara might have spoiled every other aspect of Christmas for her this year, but there was no way Eloise was going to slack in the kitchen. She didn't need her parents or a boyfriend or her stupid, bull-headed, workaholic sister. She'd have a perfect Christmas.

Even if she had to have it by herself.

Five hours, eight minutes till Christmas

Chapter 17

She felt sick. Awful. The worst human being in the world.

And watching the Disney version of *A Christmas Carol* wasn't helping. She just kept thinking she was like Scrooge and she was just as bad as him, but she wouldn't be visited by three spirits to help her change her ways overnight.

George paused the DVD. "Right. Come on. Talk to me. You've been sad and grumpy all night and you've barely said a word."

She'd told him not to ask when he'd arrived, and so far, he hadn't.

That was almost two hours ago.

Cara teared up instantly, feeling her lip wobble. She bit

181

it, hard, looking at her hands absently twisting together. "I'm the worst person. Eloise hates me."

"Why? Did you forget to buy her a present?" His smile faded quickly. "Sorry. Bad time for a joke, I guess."

"No shit," Cara muttered. "She hates me. She told me not to bother coming for Christmas."

George exclaimed, stammering, before managing to spit out, "What? Your sister? Not that I've ever met her, but I don't believe that. And it's Christmas. The season of goodwill. Whatever it is, she can't stay mad at you for long. She'll forget all about it tomorrow when you're there."

"That's just it! I told her maybe I wouldn't come, because of the weather, and I didn't know if I'd even manage to make it and my bus might be cancelled, and she just flipped. I said I'd go in a few days when all the travel services are back to normal and the snow's gone and she just screamed at me. It was awful. I'm awful. I shouldn't have said anything. I knew it'd upset her."

"So why did you? You might still make it."

"I just wanted to let her know. Prepare her. I'm already expecting to not be able to travel, so I just thought I'd warn her. I *thought* it was the right thing to do. Then we got into a fight and I called her an ungrateful bitch, and she hung up on me. Not that I blame her."

Cara had tried calling back. She'd sent messages on every app they had. Eloise was ignoring her, though. Which was fair, she guessed, but ... They always made up when they fought. And it was Christmas.

This wasn't like the usual fights they had, though. Cara got a stomach ache just thinking about it. Did Eloise really think she had it better, or think she didn't miss home sometimes? Eloise had breezed through school, university, and into a job. Cara had sat on dozens of rejection emails, staying up to the early hours of the morning sometimes filling in applications before she got even one interview. And now Eloise wanted to blame her for having to work that much harder to just be on the same level as her?

She still probably shouldn't have called her an ungrateful bitch, though.

That had been a step too far.

She was glad George was still here, to vent to. He'd been an okay distraction for the last couple of hours too.

George's dad was supposed to have come to pick him up earlier that day, but between roadworks that had blocked off one of the main routes for weeks and the ice ... it hadn't happened. George had booked himself a taxi, by some miracle, the next morning.

That's what I should've done. Booked a bloody taxi all the way up to Doncaster.

Maybe if she'd just put the effort in for Christmas, they'd have avoided the entire shit-show of a phone call.

George kissed her temple, wrapping his arms around her and pulling her closer to him. They were laid out on the sofa, Cara sitting between his legs; he tucked his face over her shoulder, next to hers.

"No use panicking about it now," he said softly, one

hand stroking the ends of her hair. "It might be nine degrees and sunshine tomorrow. The forecast is almost always wrong when it comes to snow, I swear. Eloise'll just be upset that you might not be there tomorrow, but she'll want you there. Of course she will."

"She sounded so mad ..."

"Upset," he corrected, and sounded so convinced that Cara believed him, despite the fact that he hadn't even heard the conversation. "Just wait and see in the morning, hmm? And if you're really snowed in – she can't be mad at you then."

Cara nodded.

How did he manage to do that? Make her stop worrying so much and relax her like that? It was like a magic trick.

But he was right. He had to be.

This was Eloise they were talking about. Her twin sister. They never stayed mad at each other longer than a couple of hours and, whatever it was, it always blew over and they laughed about it after.

Then again – she'd never been so downright mean to her before, and she'd never suggested missing Christmas before and been the reason Eloise would spend her favourite holiday all alone.

She won't be spending it alone, Cara told herself resolutely. *Because I'll get there. I'll spend Christmas with my sister and make sure she doesn't spend it alone. I'll make it. I'll fix this.*

George kissed her cheek and pressed play on the DVD again.

She even managed to enjoy the rest of it.

Christmas Day
6.22 a.m.

Chapter 18

It was nice to wake up with someone on Christmas Day, Eloise decided, when she rolled over and found herself facing Jamie that morning. In the split second before she'd properly woken up, she'd forgotten he was there, and smiled. He looked good when he was sleeping – even if he was drooling a little right now.

But, to be fair, he looked good all the time.

She still couldn't understand how she'd never noticed before. All that time living across the hallway from each other, hardly speaking, and he'd just been shy, and she'd been too wrapped up in Josh and then getting over Josh to even notice.

Sod Josh, she thought then. Who gave a shit about Josh?

Jamie, though: Jamie was right here, with her, and so wonderful.

Eloise kissed his nose, waking him up a little. Bleary-eyed, he blinked, sucking in a breath, smacking his lips as he lifted his head a little off the pillow. It wasn't attractive, but it was. How did he manage to do that?

"Merry Christmas," she whispered, grinning.

He mumbled something incoherent that she guessed was, "Merry Christmas."

Jamie had fallen asleep first last night; he'd stayed, the weather here and back in Nottingham only getting worse as the evening went on. Eloise felt sorry for him, but she was secretly a little glad. It had been nice to have company last night.

And it was nice to have company this morning too.

After he'd fallen asleep, she'd slipped out of bed and made up stockings for them both. She'd bought him a couple of things – token gifts, mostly: chocolates, a bobble hat, a *Game of Thrones* keyring, a set of pens designed to look like miniature lightsabers – things like that. Chucking in a couple of oranges and a mug she'd bought as a spare present in case she'd forgotten one of the teachers at school, it was enough to make up a stocking.

For her own, she'd tossed in a few random small gifts from the pile her parents had done for her.

As Jamie woke himself up, reaching over for his glasses, Eloise could hardly contain herself. Maybe it wasn't

Christmas like she'd imagined, but it was still Christmas.

Only the best damn day of the year, as far as she was concerned.

And who needed Cara? Eloise was going to have a great Christmas all by herself. (Or, with Jamie, she supposed.)

Jamie kissed her, smiling. His chin was rough against her face. "Morning."

"I made you a stocking," she announced, climbing out of bed. She pulled on her dressing gown off the wardrobe door and lifted the two stockings from the foot of the bed. "Ignore the fact that it has Cara embroidered on it. I didn't have another one."

"What – how did you –?"

"Looks like you're on Santa's Nice List this year," she told him and he laughed, running a hand through his hair. "It's only little things. And I know you want to set off early, but I just thought – it's Christmas morning, and you should have a stocking."

"More like it gave you an excuse to do one for yourself," he teased, grabbing it eagerly.

"I mean, that too."

Jamie kissed her again, this one longer, lingering a while, making her nerves fizz, sparking like live wires right under her skin.

Okay, so she was willing to admit that Christmas wasn't turning out *so* awful. So far.

They tore into their stockings, Jamie opening up one of the oranges and offering her a few segments partway

187

through. Half of Eloise's gifts were socks or bits from Body Shop, and she was thrilled to see her mum had remembered to get her some of those Neutrogena make-up wipes she loved so much. There were some earrings too, which she loved and were exactly her kind of thing. She came across a chocolate orange, whacking it on the corner of her bedside table and offering a few segments to Jamie in return.

"This is amazing," he told her, scrunching up the discarded wrapping paper into one big ball, picking it up carefully so he didn't accidentally grab a present. He kissed her again – then again, and again, smattering kisses across her cheek and nose and everywhere he could reach, leaving her giggling, grabbing his face so she could kiss him properly, his glasses squashing against her face and skewing sideways.

"Seriously, thank you. This was a perfect start to a crappy sort of Christmas Day."

"My thoughts exactly."

"I'm going to make some tea. Do you want me to make some breakfast? I know you've got eggs and stuff in – what do you say to poached eggs? And bacon sandwiches like you said you normally have, right?"

"That's sweet," she laughed, "but I think I'll just have some toast. I'm not actually feeling that hungry."

Jamie chuckled, rolling halfway over her. His glasses slipped off his nose a little, hair tickling her face. "I can think of one way to work up an appetite ..."

"I thought you were meant to be on the road early?"

He looked over at the clock. "I've got time."

"Er, Eloise?"

She laughed. It wasn't like he hadn't seen her naked, but he knocked while she was in the shower. She didn't know why she found that so funny.

"What?"

"You might want to look outside."

Eloise frowned, wondering what that was meant to mean, and why it was so urgent, and walked to the other end of the bath, away from the warmth of the shower head, to peek under the roller blind covering the window.

Snow.

So. Much. Fucking. *Snow*.

"Looks like a white Christmas after all," Jamie called through the door.

So it did.

How was Jamie going to get home? How was Cara going to get here? (Not, Eloise reminded herself quickly, that she was even going to bother coming, after their fight yesterday.) She couldn't help but wonder, though: Was she snowed in in London? Was it this bad just on their road or was it covering the whole town, the whole city? They weren't supposed to have that much snow.

The cars looked like misshapen marshmallows, completely covered by it. You couldn't see the road or the pavement or even tell where the two met. Eloise could see down the hill slightly, across their little suburb, and all she saw were white roofs and white roads and white trees and white, white, *white*.

Why, of all years, did this one have to be a white Christmas? Literally any other year she'd have been home with her parents, and Cara, and it wouldn't even have mattered. It would've only made the day so much more magical.

And it *did* look magical. Sparkling in the pale light and streetlamps, the world that bit more silent than it usually was at this time of the morning.

Eloise loved the snow. The other day she'd been out walking in it, making little snowmen by herself and sending Cara Snapchats, singing lines from *Do You Want to Build a Snowman?* over them.

But not today.

Why did it have to be today?

She finished her shower, her mood having taken a total dip, and her mouth was downturned when she left the bathroom, dressing gown on and hair wrapped in a towel. Jamie was making breakfast – poached eggs and toast with a side of bacon – and his face mirrored hers.

"What are you going to do?" she asked him quietly.

"I have no idea."

"I've got a shovel. We could try dig your car a path to the main road. It might not be so thick there."

"Maybe." He sighed. "Bloody typical. It's not even

snowing at home any more. The roads aren't too bad there now, where people have been going out on them."

She bit her lip, not knowing what to say, except, "I'm sorry. I know it sucks not spending Christmas the way you planned."

"What's Cara going to do?"

Eloise shrugged. She'd text everyone good morning and Happy Christmas, and had gone in the shower before anybody replied. Even if they hadn't argued like that yesterday, she doubted Cara would be coming today. Or tomorrow. Or even this weekend, probably, knowing her. She'd want to stay and work.

"Well," she said then, trying to find the bright side, "at least we've got a turkey dinner."

Christmas Day
6.31 a.m.

Chapter 19

*B*ang!
    Something light fell across her face and hair as she shot bolt upright, breathless, heart contracting.

George laughed at her, holding a party popper in his hand, the stringy paper contents of which were currently on top of her head. "Merry Christmas!"

She threw a cushion at him. "That's no way to wake someone up! You could've given me a heart attack!"

"Oh, come on. You can't have Christmas without party poppers!"

"Uh, we can, and we do. They're strictly a New Year's Eve kind of thing as far as my family are concerned."

"Pfft. You're all wrong."

He sat on the bed beside her, kissing her. Cara leant up into it, smiling against his lips. "Merry Christmas to you too," she murmured, then drew back to shove at him playfully. "Even if you did almost give me a heart attack. What time is it, anyway? I didn't hear the alarm go off."

They both had to be up and out early to get back to their families for Christmas so she'd set an alarm for seven. She didn't exactly have to get dressed up to sit on a bus for the next few hours. She might slap on a little make-up once she got to Eloise's, though, for whatever photos they took to post on Instagram and send to their parents.

If she even decided to go to Eloise's.

"It's half six. I know, I *know*, it's early, but I wanted to make sure I gave you your present before I left."

"*Ooh*. Now I'm awake. Always lead with the presents, George, FYI. Not the party poppers."

"What was I meant to do? Waft the wrapping paper under your nose like smelling salts?"

She pulled a face, pretending to mull it over. "That would've worked, yeah."

George laughed, moving around to his bags pushed against one wall of her room and pulling out her gift. It was small, boxy. He sat on top of the covers, cross-legged on his side of the bed, to hand it to her.

"No, no, wait! I've got to get yours first!"

She reached into her bedside drawer for it, handing it over. A jumper she thought would suit him (and hoped would fit), and she'd got him a box of coffees he could use in his coffee machine at home. They were nothing exciting, but she felt they were thoughtful gifts all the same.

He seemed to think so too, grinning broadly once he'd opened them, approving of the coffee beans and yanking his T-shirt off to try on the jumper. She was relieved to see it fitted, having stammered about the gift receipt and how she wouldn't be offended if he didn't like it and wanted to return it or exchange it.

He shut her up with a swift peck on the lips. "I love it. Thanks, Cara."

She opened her gift next. It was bookish, which made her wonder, because they'd never really talked that much about books (aside from when she was banging on about her book club).

It was a diary. A planner, with a section for budgeting and to-do lists and stickers and Post-it notes. It was a little bulky, sure, but it would cover every aspect of her life.

"I know you keep saying you can't find an app for organising your life, so I figured you could try this."

"It's perfect." It was: she loved it. He'd definitely outdone her on the thoughtful gift front, by miles. Throwing her arms around him, she kissed him, nuzzling her face against his and beaming. "But you know you didn't have to get me anything. Honestly. I'd have been happy with just you."

"Are you trying to use Mariah Carey to sound cute?"

She hadn't meant to. She was just being honest. But it made her giggle when he pointed it out, and she poked her tongue out at him. George was smiling at her, hair a mess after he'd washed it and not styled it last night – she was so used to seeing it combed back and so neat that she always forgot it looked any other way. He was wearing reindeer boxer shorts and still had the new jumper she'd bought him on, his fingers absently stroking across hers.

Cara opened her mouth, then shut it again.

They'd only been properly dating for a few weeks. Wasn't it too early to be saying stuff like that? Wouldn't she just look like a fool if she said it this early on?

Eloise would be telling her no, quoting that bit of *Love Actually* at her when Natalie declares her love for the Prime Minister in her Christmas card to him; she'd be encouraging her to tell him. Just blurt it out already.

But Cara had never been in love before. She'd never particularly *done* relationships before George. And she was so frightened of screwing it up and losing him.

He said something, and she was so wrapped up in her own head that she missed it. Blinked at him. "Huh? What was that?"

He chuckled, but shifted, a little uncomfortable. "I can't tell if you genuinely didn't hear me or you're just taking the piss."

"Genuinely didn't hear. Sorry. In a world of my own."

"I said, I think I love you. No – actually, you know what? Sod it. There's no *think* about it. I do love you. I love your always-chipped nail varnish you're always too busy to fix and the way you get so excited when you talk about your job and I love you despite the fact you think

Phoebe and Joey should have ended up together in *Friends*."

She laughed. "That's so generous of you."

Cara kissed him. Hand on his cheek, nose squashed against his, enjoying the shiver he sent down her spine when he kissed her back. She could never get tired of kissing him.

"Is this the part where I tell you I love you too?"

"Not if you don't mean it." He blinked a few times, words a little breathless from all the kissing.

"It's a good thing I do mean it, then," she told him. Then, the words sounding strange coming out of her mouth and in her voice and so matter-of-fact, but feeling like the most wonderful and normal thing in the world to say to him, Cara said, "I love you."

"And here I thought today couldn't get better than those coffee beans."

This wasn't happening.

This couldn't be happening.

Her bus was running. Diverted, only going to Nottingham, but it was still running. She was on it now – had been for about an hour. There hadn't been any more snow in the last couple of days, even though they'd been forecast some, thank God. Even the ice had thawed out a little.

George had managed to get home: his taxi had picked him up from Cara's that morning, just before she'd left for the bus station, and after a very, very long kiss goodbye, and a few more giggled and giddy 'I love you's.

Cara still wasn't convinced Eloise would even want her there, but she'd received a perky-sounding 'Merry Christmas!' text that morning, along with an essay of how Jamie had ended up staying the night again and she'd done them both stockings. Evidently, Eloise wasn't too mad at her.

Admittedly, those had all been in their little family group WhatsApp, but still. Cara was included on them.

And none of it meant she'd want her there, but Cara had to take the chance she would. It was her fault Eloise would be spending it alone, after all.

And waking up next to George that morning, Cara had to admit to herself that she didn't really want to spend the day alone either. And that she'd really, really screwed up.

But now Eloise was on the phone, voice high and fast and panicky, words running into each other so much that Cara was having a hard time keeping up with her.

Eloise was snowed in.

Cara had called to apologise and say she was on her way, she'd been such an idiot, but Eloise hadn't seemed to care. She'd barely drawn breath, never mind acknowledged their argument.

There was snow all across the Midlands and up north, Eloise was telling her, as if Cara hadn't already seen when she'd checked her phone that morning.

"How are you even going to get here? Isn't your coach cancelled? What are you going to do? Where are you going? Were you going to get a taxi?"

"Breathe," Cara told her. "The one I'm on now goes as far as Nottingham. Then there's meant to be a bus going up to Newcastle I'll transfer onto. It's supposed to be coming through Doncaster, then."

"Well, I doubt it'll get very far, but even if it does – how are you going to manage to get to mine from the bus station? I'm completely snowed in. Jamie's gone to clear the snow off his car and see if he can get anywhere, but I really don't think it's going to happen. He walked down to the main road and even that's all snowed over. Nobody's driving out anywhere."

"I was going to get a taxi," Cara said absently, but it was clear that wouldn't be happening. She'd be lucky to even get into the town centre to the bus station, by the sounds of it.

"I'm so sorry, Cara, I'm so sorry, I didn't even think to look out the window this morning. We weren't expecting snow, and I just didn't even think to check, and – oh, God, I feel awful. I should've text before you got on the bus so you'd know not to come. Are you going to be able to get another one back to London? I don't think any trains are running today. Do you want me to go online and look for you?"

"No, no, that's okay," Cara said, "I've got loads of signal and battery, and my portable charger. I can look."

"Are you sure? I'm so sorry!"

"Why are you sorry? I'm the one who was being stingy and grumpy enough to not want to travel yesterday. Or even on the weekend. If I'd taken some time off work – or even just worked remotely, I'd have been there for Christmas. And I should've. And I'm the one who gave Mum and Dad the stupid idea to go abroad and –"

"Oh, have you spoken to them yet this morning? I said we'd FaceTime later, both of us, when you got here, but that was before I saw the snow. God, see, if Mum and Dad had stayed home, you'd be fine. You could just go straight home!"

"Shoot. I should've brought my key, shouldn't I? Could've at least stayed there for the night or something. Shit, I didn't even think about that. And no, I text Dad to say I was on the bus and stuff. Do you want to go ahead and ring them now? I'll talk to them later, when I'm not on the bus."

"Okay."

Cara and Eloise both hesitated for a second before –

"I'm sorry."

They spoke at the same time, and then paused again and laughed.

"Don't even," said Cara. "It's not your fault. Unless you've suddenly switched roles and now you're Elsa and you're genuinely the reason for this shitstorm. I mean, snow-storm."

"No, I'm still Anna. And that was funny. And you don't need to be sorry either."

"I really do. I shouldn't have said that about Josh, or about you being ungrateful. I didn't mean it."

"Yeah, I know," she said quietly, a little unconvinced. "I shouldn't have kept going on at you about taking time off. I know how much this promotion means to you."

"Truce?"

"Truce."

"Text me and let me know what happens with Jamie," Cara said.

"Alright. And let me know what happens when you get to the bus station at Nottingham, and what's going on?"

"Will do."

They said goodbye and hung up, Cara's leg bouncing and her phone bouncing on her knee.

She had to get to Eloise.

One way or another.

She'd get there.

Christmas Day
11.20 a.m.

Chapter 20

Alright, so it wasn't the *worst* Christmas she could've imagined. Jamie was here, which made a huge difference.

And it wasn't like he was being grumpy or grouchy or the moody neighbour she was so used to knowing – he wasn't complaining. If anything, he seemed quite happy to watch her DVD of *Fantastic Beasts and Where to Find Them*, which she couldn't believe he'd still not seen – although he did keep asking questions that she pointed out he'd already know the answers to if he'd actually read the books. (She still wasn't over that.)

Eloise knew this wasn't where he wanted to be today though. He'd FaceTimed his family and even introduced her to them, and them to her, catching her arm and forcing the iPad into her hands when she'd tried to back out of the room to give him some peace and quiet.

Video chat wasn't the same, though. She would attest to that, having called her parents while he was out shovelling snow away from his car, putting on a brave face and not whining or crying or anything like that because the snow had ruined Christmas.

(And of all the things that might have ruined the day, with everything that had gone on the last few weeks. *Snow*. The most magical, festive thing of all. It was the icing on the cake.)

(Or on the rooftops, she guessed.)

Jamie wasn't complaining, but she knew he wished he was at home with his family.

Same as she wished Cara were here.

"What time do you want to do dinner?" she asked him.

"Whenever you like. You're the one cooking."

"There's not much to cook. Gravy to reheat and then I'll just bung them in the microwave for a few minutes."

"I still can't believe you do your own gravy. Not even a Bisto mix."

"You don't know how to make gravy?"

"Nope. My dad taught me how to boil an egg when I was twelve, though."

Eloise rolled her eyes. "Unbelievable."

"Gravy's pretty niche. I do a good stroganoff. And risotto. I'm *very* good at risotto. I made bread from scratch a couple of times too, and that wasn't half bad. But, honest to God – you're the only person I know who can actually make gravy," he said, grabbing another Dairy Milk out of the tub of Heroes, adding the wrapping to the growing pile on his lap.

"You'll be too full of chocolate to eat," she said, sounding exactly like her dad.

Jamie laughed. "That's the sort of thing my mum would say. It's Christmas. I swear the day does something to you. Your stomach just *knows*. Any other day of the year – you're right, I'd be too full to eat dinner. I'd be too full from breakfast to be eating all this now. But my stomach knows what day it is. I bet I could eat a whole turkey if I wanted to. Like Joey in that episode of *Friends*."

"That's exactly what I'm picturing." She laughed and dragged herself out of the corner of the sofa, swinging her legs down from where her feet had been balanced on Jamie's knees. She gathered up the Heroes wrappers from both of them. "It's too early for dinner yet. Tea and biccies?"

"I could definitely do tea and biccies."

She got the good biscuits out of the cupboard, from the little food package her parents had put together for her and Cara, and checked her phone while the kettle boiled. Nothing from Cara.

Eloise rang her. "Are you on a bus back to London?"

"Hello to you too. And yeah, I'm on a bus."

"Oh, good. I was worried you'd have to find somewhere to stay and –"

205

"And there'd be no room at the Premier Inn?" Cara laughed. "Don't worry about me, hon, I'm fine. How's Mr Darcy doing? This is a very couple-y thing to be doing when you're not a proper couple, you know."

Eloise felt herself blushing, because Cara was only saying what she'd been thinking herself. Sniffing, she said, "He's fine, thanks. We're watching a film. I'll do dinner later. And, for your information, that is no longer the case. He asked me to be his girlfriend. Properly, you know."

"Wait, what? What! As of when?"

"As of yesterday. It was all very spur-of-the-moment and adorable and of course I told him he was daft."

Cara squealed down the phone. "Did Mr Darcy not think to ask our father's permission first? Mama will be beside herself. You know, it is a truth –"

"Please shut up."

"What time are you doing dinner?"

"Er, probably one. When the film's finished."

"What're you watching? I'm stuck with the Netflix downloads on my phone, and I forgot to download anything new. So I'm watching the same three episodes of *Jane the Virgin* over and over."

They talked a while longer, Eloise hanging up when the tea was made. She felt uneasy. It hadn't helped, calling Cara. Their argument had blown over, surprisingly, and she was glad, but ... It only made her miss her more.

They should've been spending the day together, not miles apart. Her sister shouldn't have been spending half her day travelling back and forth on a bus. It wasn't fair. It wasn't right, not today.

Eloise looked out of the window.

It was snowing again.

Christmas Day
12.26 p.m.

Chapter 21

The bus made it to Doncaster town centre – barely.

It had taken at least an hour longer than it should've as they'd got closer to the city, but some of the roads were fairly clear; Cara guessed there were a lot of people who'd insisted on driving today, despite the snow.

The bus station itself was pretty snowed under, though, so the bus ended up pulling in somewhere off the main road near the town. A handful of other people got off, splitting in different directions. Cara shouldered her rucksack and heaved her duffel bag over her bulky coat, staggering a little. God, she knew she should've just had Eloise's gifts sent directly to her. And she was starting to wish she'd spent some goddamn money on a suitcase.

And snow shoes.

And like, a balaclava. The cold made her eyes water and she buried the bottom half of her face in her scarf, shoulders hunching up.

Between the hat and scarf, giant coat and the Christmas jumper she was wearing under it, and the bags, Cara felt like she waddled the entire way to the taxi rank, blindly following a couple with bags who were heading through town.

It was so quiet.

Quiet because nobody was around, and because of the snow. Cara had been through the town centre before, when she'd been to visit Eloise, but it looked foreign in this light. New and sparkling. The snow was a couple of inches thick, crunching under her feet as she struggled to make headway.

Sunshine was trying to get through the clouds, at least. She could cross her fingers and hope that by some miracle it'd all melt in the next ten minutes.

Her phone buzzed in her pocket, and Cara ignored it for once. It definitely wouldn't be work: *nobody* was working today to be emailing her. It was probably a text from a friend saying Happy Christmas or Eloise asking if she'd got back to London yet.

The couple ahead of her got into a taxi just as she got to the road. There were two other taxis idling on the side of the road; both the drivers were standing under a bus shelter, smoking.

Cara waddled towards them, pulling off one of her gloves and regretting it immediately: her hand would drop off from frostbite in about twenty seconds. God, it was cold. She ignored the text from Eloise and the few other notifications on her screen to pull up her Notes app, finding the one with Eloise's address.

"Alright, love?"

She turned her phone towards the driver who'd spoken. "I'm trying to get here?"

The driver stubbed out his cigarette under a heavy snow-friendly shoe. Cara's own toes were cramping and cold and damp through her trainers. She really needed to get some proper shoes for this kind of weather.

He puffed his cheeks out, head shaking in a way that made her stomach sink.

"Please." Cara was mortified when her voice cracked. Her fingers gripped the phone a little tighter, shaking from the cold. "What's the fare? I'll pay extra."

Both the drivers laughed. "Love, the prices are already jacked up because it's Christmas."

"I know, but – I'm trying to get to my sister. The roads must be safe enough if you're out here waiting for customers, right?"

"I'll get you as close as I can," the driver said, not looking totally convinced. He blipped open the car, opening the boot. "But I'm not gonna risk my car getting stuck if the roads aren't clear enough, alright?"

"Yes, yes, that's fine. Thank you. Thank you so much."

"Here, give me those bags. Let's get you home for Christmas, eh?"

The taxi driver got her to the outskirts of the village, yanking on the handbrake and turning to her with a sigh and a face full of sympathy.

"Sorry, love, but I can't do much better than that. Looks like hardly anybody's been in and out of the village today – at least by car."

"No, this is great. This is fine. Thank you so much." Cara checked the meter, and dug into her rucksack for her purse. She was glad she'd thought to take out cash and bring it along; usually she just had an emergency twenty-pound note and her cards. She'd originally planned on getting to town and having Eloise pick her up.

"Oh, no, look – don't worry about that," the driver said when she cleaned out her purse, emergency twenty-pound note and all, to give him an extra few quid and the odd change on top of the fare. He tried to pass her back one of the twenties, but Cara was already opening the door.

"I didn't drive you because you said you'd pay me extra. It's Christmas," the driver told her. "You're just trying to get to your family."

"Exactly," she replied, smiling, "it's Christmas."

He laughed, getting out to help with her bag in the boot. "Don't tell me – you were visited by three ghosts last night and now you're determined to do a little good in the world."

Cara took the duffel bag, wrestling it over her body and

hoisting her rucksack back into place. "Something like that. Merry Christmas."

"And to you."

"Safe driving," she told him, and started to haul ass down the road and towards Eloise's.

Cara knew the village a little: there was a corner shop she and Eloise had walked to a couple of times, and she vaguely knew her way through to the flats. She knew it would have been maybe a fifteen, twenty-minute walk to Eloise's flat – in normal circumstances.

And her sister would be doing Christmas dinner any time now.

She wanted to get there just before that. Cara had visions of showing up just before Eloise sat down to Christmas dinner, surprising her just in time, so they could eat together, and it would all be perfect and idyllic and like something out of a Hallmark movie.

She'd had a lot of time on those buses to think that over.

Less time to actually make it happen, she knew; which was why she gritted her teeth, put her head down against the cold and ploughed through the snow, her long coat and the duffel bag hitting her thigh hindering her from lifting her knees too high.

This was the most intense workout she'd had in months.

Cara did her best not to get distracted by the other Hallmark-worthy scenes in the houses she was passing. Kids (and teenagers and adults and whole families) were out playing in their front gardens in the snow, building

213

snowmen, and open curtains and blinds let her glance into a few homes to see them already sitting down to dinner. A few houses where the kids were running around playing with new toys or unwrapping more presents.

She loved the Christmas trees lit up in the houses.

She'd passed the corner shop and knew it wasn't far now, but she had to stop, breathing hard, swinging the duffel bag around to sit the other way across her body. She was sweating under all these layers, had to pull off the hat and wipe her gloved hand across her forehead. She felt gross. Her lungs burned and she had a stitch. Her legs were killing her.

Why was walking through the snow this hard? She'd be toned as hell by the time she actually made it to Eloise.

And damn, there was a whole hill to climb before she actually got to the flats.

Cara pulled one of her gloves off with her teeth, getting her phone back out. She really had to catch her breath. How did people do that valiant-looking run through the snow in the movies? How did *anybody* run through snow, *ever*? It was like, the biggest con ever.

There was another text from Eloise, and a missed call, and a text from George too.

She opened that one.

Just getting ready to all sit down for dinner. How are things going with you? Did you manage to get to Eloise yet?

Cara chanced calling him.

He answered on the second ring. "Alright? Are you with Eloise now?"

"Er, almost. I'm not far."

"Why are you breathing so heavy? You sound like a serial killer."

"I'm just incredibly unfit," she confessed. Way more so than she'd realised. That ab class she went to once a week with Jen was so not doing it. "I'm walking."

"From where?"

"Just through the village. God, it's a big village. Do you know how big this village is? It's tiny on Google Maps but it's all a lie."

George laughed down the phone. She could hear chatter in the background, and something on the TV. The sound of a cracker being pulled and laughter.

"I'm not interrupting your dinner, am I?"

"Oh, no! My mum's just doing the gravy now. It's all ... weirdly cosy. No fighting. I think Lina's accident gave us all a good scare. I've got a few minutes. So you're walking to your sister's? That's dedication."

"I'm still not convinced she'll want me there."

"Just say you're right: what's she going to do? Turn you out into the snow?"

Probably with a comment that I can build my own ice palace to hide out in, Cara thought. She said, "Okay. Well. I'll let you know if that happens and then, if I freeze to death, you'll know why. I'll let you get back to your family.

I don't want to make you late for dinner. It'll ruin the whole hardworking, wholesome vibe I've got going for a first impression."

George laughed again. "Good luck not freezing to death."

Breath back and stitch mostly gone, Cara said goodbye and looked around, leaning her head back. She definitely needed a hot shower when she got to Eloise's; her shoulders and neck were killing her from carrying these bloody bags.

Cara looked at the house she was standing outside.

No lights on, no movement, no open windows and excited voices.

She was half-expecting to see the curtains wide open like some of the other houses, another family just like hers at the table with their dinner, two smiling girls and their parents, exactly like they would've all been today if she hadn't given her parents the idea to go on holiday or if she had just travelled up this weekend. She'd ruined Christmas, single-handedly.

She had to make it right.

Christmas Day
1.02 p.m.

Chapter 22

Dinner was dished out. Eloise had put together two heaped plates from the food she'd prepared yesterday, and was warming gravy on the stove. Jamie had offered to help, but she'd told him she had this all handled.

Right now, he was wrapping tinsel around her like a feather boa, belting along to *Jingle Bell Rock* which was playing over her mini Bluetooth speaker.

Eloise laughed, trying to shake him off. "You'll get tinsel in the gravy."

"It'll add a little extra something. A little sparkle."

She laughed again, grinning over her shoulder. Jamie didn't have a Christmas jumper (something she found absolutely scandalous) but he'd made up for it now, tying

217

some tinsel around his head and wearing another strand around his neck. A bauble hung from his ear, swinging violently as he danced around and threatening to shoot off somewhere at any second.

"Oh, come on! Leave that!" He reached past her, turning the hob off and grabbing her hands when she tried to protest, moving her arms around. "Dance with me."

"Two minutes ago you were the one whinging about how hungry you were."

"And now I want to dance. Come on." He spun her around, singing along again.

"Wait."

Eloise pushed his arms away, head tilting, trying to listen over the music.

"There."

She was sure she'd heard it again. A knock.

"I swear someone just knocked the door."

Eloise reached for her phone, hitting pause on the music.

"It was probably just someone upstairs, dropping something."

"No, I ... Mind the gravy."

Someone was singing. *Good King Wenceslas*. It sounded like a girl, but as if she was putting on a voice. Maybe it was the little girl from downstairs and she wanted to go carol singing, sponge some mince pies off the neighbours or something. Or maybe it was just one of the neighbours coming round to say Happy Christmas. Possibly after a little too much wine.

Eloise brushed past Jamie, his face just as confused as she felt, as she opened the door.

She shrieked, hands flapping. It was just as well she wasn't holding anything. Especially her phone. It probably would've flown out at the wall, the way her hands jerked. Eloise cried out again, clapping her hands over her mouth.

She started to tear up.

Cara laughed, a watery, shaky kind of sound, and she shrugged, hands waving around her hips just as jerkily and excited as Eloise's were.

She was bundled up completely in her big winter coat, a thick woollen scarf that matched her bobble hat and the black leather gloves they'd both got from their aunt and uncle last Christmas. Cara's face was bright pink; tendrils of hair stuck to her face. Her jeans were damp and flecked with a little snow and her shoes were dripping on the carpet.

"Surprise!"

"What the – what are you ...? How did y– I thought you were going back to London!"

Cara laughed again, the sound brighter and less wobbly this time. "I couldn't leave my little sister on her own for Christmas, could I? Even if you are with your booty call. Boyfriend. Whatever the hell you wanna call him. He doesn't count. Not as much as I do, anyway."

"Little sister? Excuse you. Thirteen minutes and I'm definitely the more mature of both of us."

"Liar, liar, pants on fire."

"You're literally proving my point."

"You're the one keeping me out on the doorstep." Cara sniffed, wiggling her nose. "You gonna let me in? I just walked all the way through your bloody village in shoes that apparently aren't made for this weather."

"Oh, God, yeah, come – come in. I ... I can't believe you're here!"

Cara had barely waddled through the doorway when Eloise squealed again, throwing her arms around her sister. She thought Cara tried to hug her back, but it was kind of hard to tell: she could barely move her arms between the coat and the bags.

Jamie was still loitering in the kitchen doorway, leaning against it with his ankles and arms crossed. "So this is the famous Cara."

Eloise stepped back. Cara grinned at him, pulling her hat off. "Hiya. Alright?"

Jamie looked at Eloise. "Did you tell your sister I'm your booty call? Do you make up stockings for all your booty calls?"

"Only the good ones."

He laughed.

"I'd hug you," Cara said, "but it's hard to do anything in this marshmallow suit. El, you mind if I take a shower? And I think I need to nick one of your Christmas jumpers. This one's probably all sweaty and gross. Do you have any idea how hard it is to walk all that way in the snow?"

"Think you can wait another half hour for dinner?" Eloise asked Jamie.

"Only if I can have another mince pie in the meantime."

She laughed. "You don't have to ask just because my sister's here. It's not like you haven't been helping yourself to them all day."

Jamie kissed her cheek. "Thank yooooou. Do you want some tea, Cara? Milk? Sugar?"

"I like this one," she told Eloise, winking. "Josh *never* offered to make me tea, and he was around for *years*. Milk, no sugar please, thanks."

"Roger that, boss." Jamie mock-saluted her and went back to the kitchen; Cara dragged herself after Eloise to the bedroom, where she unravelled herself from her bags and peeled off her coat and soaked shoes, sighing in relief. Eloise was rooting through her wardrobe for her guest towels.

"How did you even get here?"

Cara told her while she peeled off wet socks and wiggled out of her jumper and jeans and flopped onto the end of the bed in her thermal vest and knickers – how she'd gotten another bus up to town, got a taxi, walked through the village. It was a little less epic than Eloise expected, but the way Cara told it was every bit as heroic and wonderful as she felt it was. Her eyes shone as she spoke, and when she said that she'd buzzed the intercom for one of the neighbours, asking to be let in so she could surprise her sister, Eloise let out a sob before she even knew she was crying.

221

Cara squeezed her hand. "Oi. Pull it together. You'll ruin your make-up. Get all that glittery eye-shadow in your eyes."

Eloise laughed weakly, wiping her fingertips gently at the corners of her eyes. "I just can't believe you've come. What about work? What if you can't get back till next week?"

"They'll just have to manage without me," Cara declared. Eloise gasped in shock before her sister added, "But I have my phone. And my MacBook. I can do some work if I need to."

Eloise wasn't even mad. She just shoved Cara's shoulder and laughed, throwing the towel at her head. "Don't use all my body wash or you're not getting any turkey."

Christmas Day
9.34 p.m.

Chapter 23

Eloise groaned from the other end of the sofa. "I'm so full. So full."

She reached for the tin of Quality Street, fishing through them and pulling out an empty wrapper.

"What kind of monster –"

"Bet it was Jamie," Cara said quickly. Too quickly, obviously, since Eloise narrowed her eyes at her.

"Jamie who says he doesn't like the whole nut ones? You fiend. Inciting such anarchy. I let you into my home, give you dinner, on Christmas Day, and this is how you repay me. Despicable. Utterly and truly despicable."

"Chuck us one," Cara said, not bothering to apologise, and Eloise tossed a handful at her – a little viciously, and they scattered across her lap, one falling to the floor. She was stuffed too: Eloise had a fridge packed full of leftovers from the massive Christmas dinner she'd cooked (that probably could've fed half the village) as well as party food. They'd had a mish-mash tea of sausage rolls and turkey sandwiches, crisps and duck spring rolls and a block of cheese with cranberries in it.

Didn't stop either of them eating more chocolates, of course.

If you couldn't eat ten days' worth of your daily calories in one day on Christmas, when could you?

Cara wondered if there were any mince pies left. And then remembered the mini cheesecake bites she'd spied in the fridge.

Jamie had left earlier that afternoon. A few people had ventured out after lunch, and Eloise had helped him shovel himself out of his parking spot. The roads had cleared up for him back home, and the ones here weren't so bad now it was later in the day and more people had been driving. He'd text Eloise a couple of hours before to say he'd got home safe. It had taken him at least twice as long as it should've, but he was back with his family for Christmas.

And much as Cara had liked him, and liked the way he and Eloise looked at each other with big, gooey eyes and soppy smiles, she was kind of glad he'd left. It wasn't that she'd felt like a third wheel or anything, but –

But she kind of had, a couple of times, and it was nice

that she got to spend the last few hours of Christmas Day with her sister.

Plus, it had felt a bit awkward to open all their presents when Jamie had nothing to open. Eloise had already opened half of hers, not having expected Cara at all and wanting to save the other half for the afternoon so she had something else to look forward to.

A restraint Cara would never have displayed herself.

It was a miracle she'd not torn open her presents from Jen right there in the Tube station the other day. (Jen had only been the best friend ever, getting her all the little things she could need for a night in – a small bottle of wine, fuzzy socks, a face mask, nail varnish and another romantic festive novel.)

After Jamie had left, she'd broached the subject of their argument again, still wanting to apologise. She honestly hadn't realised Eloise felt so homesick, and Eloise admitted she was stunned to hear Cara had always felt like she had to work so hard just to keep up, she'd never realised. They didn't quite manage to laugh about it, but at least they'd cleared the air.

They'd been on FaceTime to their parents just before dinner – briefly, to show off Cara's big surprise and the fact she'd actually made it, struggled through all that snow and disruption and been, like, literally, the best present Eloise had ever had. ("But that Ted Baker tote bag was so gorgeous, Mum, I loved that too!")

They'd video chatted them again in the afternoon,

when Jamie was gone and all the presents were opened, talking for almost an hour that time. Cara had stolen the iPad to show off how full Eloise's fridge and cupboards were, which had made their dad laugh for a few minutes.

"Well, just as well, since you're snowed in."

"*Funny*."

Their parents had wanted to hear about their day for ages, but then, once Cara had asked about their day and the hotel and the beach, they'd gushed non-stop, barely pausing for breath, beaming smiles on their faces as they told them how, at dinner, spontaneous carol singing had broken out and everyone had joined in and it was just so sweet, they wished they'd thought to film it, and how there were people sunbathing in Santa hats (which they did snap a discreet picture of to email them) and that they were going to the bar that evening for drinks with some of the other couples they'd met around the hotel.

"I'm so glad you're having such a great time," Cara said, meaning it.

Eloise, beside her, gulped. "Do you think … you'll go back next year? Or somewhere different, or something?"

"Oh, I doubt it!" Their mum laughed. "It's been a bit strange not having our usual day. And we've missed you girls too much. Maybe in a few years, don't you think, David? But no, darling, we're not going to make it an annual thing. Don't worry."

The relief as Eloise sighed and smiled at the camera was palpable; Cara felt Eloise's whole body relax next to her. "Okay, good. Because, nice as today has been, I really don't want to have to put up with Miss Scrooge again next year and worry about spending the day on my own. It's only because of the snow I didn't, which was a total fluke."

"Oi, I'll have you know I don't even have my work computer with me."

"And how many times did you check your emails on your phone today?"

Cara scrunched up her nose. "Twice. But, in my defence, that was on the bus, and it was out of boredom. Mostly."

She expected some kind of huffy lecture from her sister, but Eloise only laughed.

Now, she asked, "When are you planning to go back?"

"Well, if this snow shifts, I guess I'll be on my bus back tomorrow afternoon, but ... I don't know. Now I'm here I feel like I should just stay through the weekend. I'm supposed to work Friday and Monday."

"I bet if you told your boss you were snowed in they'd let you off. I bet if you just asked for the last-minute holiday they'd give it you. You could stay for New Year's Eve then and we could go out somewhere, or go back home if the weather's alright, spend it with Mum and Dad. Go back on the first. That's bank holiday anyway. You could borrow some of my clothes if you need."

Cara considered it. Thought about how most of the work she'd be doing was available through her emails or could be done from her own laptop if she needed, and she did have loads of holiday left for this year ...

They could go out for New Year's Eve. Maybe George could come up too. The four of them could go out for some cute double-date kind of thing, and they could all hang out in a too-crowded too-loud pub somewhere getting pissed on prosecco that cost too much and staggering into taxis well past midnight, she and Eloise in dresses and shoes that were in no way appropriate for this kind of weather. Eloise could stay in Jamie's flat and she and George could stay here, save on a hotel; she knew Eloise was enough of a pushover and too much of a hostess to say no to that.

It was tempting.

Only –

"I don't have enough knickers."

Eloise laughed, throwing another chocolate at her head, Cara defending herself before fishing down the side of the sofa to retrieve it.

"Maybe you don't have these in London, but here I have this magical contraption, and it's called ... *a washing machine*."

"Well ..." Cara unwrapped the caramel, popping it in her mouth and pretending to mull it over. "I guess it can't hurt to ask."

To: marcus.harris@klikit.com
Subject: Snow day???

Hey Marcus (Merry Christmas!)

*Just wanted to let you know I managed to get up to see
my sister but the snow is awful up here – not sure I'll
manage to get back to be in the office Friday. I know
it's short notice (and it'll probably be Friday before you
check your emails) but wondered if there's any chance
of me taking a couple of days off and being back in the
office on the second? I can do some work remotely too.*

Thanks,
Cara

To: cara.bells@klikit.com
Subject: RE: Snow day???

*C – WHO IS ON THEIR EMAILS ON XMAS DAY?
IT'S HOLIDAY. GO EAT SOME MINCE PIES AND
GET MERRY ON BAILEYS.*

(I don't count.)

*No problem if you want to take the time off – and
definitely don't worry about rushing back for Friday if
the weather's that bad. I'd rather have my staff safe and*

*late back to work than out on the roads when it's that
dangerous. See you on the second!*

M

Cara kicked Eloise's leg. She was half-asleep, eyes drooping,
fist propping her head up, mouth gawping open as she
tried not to fall asleep watching *Home Alone 2*.

"Marcus replied."

That woke her up. Cara had only emailed him about
twenty minutes before.

"That was fast. Who checks their emails on Christmas
Day? Have you been mentoring him in how to let work
totally consume your life?"

"It's bad news."

Her face fell, green eyes looking a little tearful. Eloise's
mouth slipped into a small pout. "Oh," she said quietly.

"You have to put up with me stealing your clothes for
a few days."

It took a moment to register, but Eloise shot bolt upright,
almost knocking her empty wine glass that was lying on
her lap to the floor. "What? Really? You're staying through
New Year's?"

Cara waggled the phone at her, beaming. She'd expected
Marcus to say as much, but it was only now he had that
she realised that was exactly what she wanted: to have a
few days taking it easy, hanging out with her sister,
spending New Year's Eve with her.

Eloise squealed, stretching across the sofa to hug Cara, who was laughing and couldn't seem to get the huge grin off her face.

She was about to say something when the TV said it for her:

"*Merry Christmas, ya filthy animal.*"

Eloise's smile was just as big as hers as she let go and nestled back into her corner of the sofa. "You know, if we do New Year's here, you should invite George up. Jamie'll probably be back. That could be cute. And I'll finally get to meet Saint George."

"I can ask him."

"I know I wasn't looking forward to it," Eloise said then, smiling at the TV, "but this is definitely the best Christmas ever."

It really, really was.

Acknowledgements

I live for Christmas, so it was only a matter of time before I turned my writing efforts to a Christmassy book. I'm all for keeping the spirit alive all year round like a reformed Scrooge, but even I was finding it weird to be watching Love Actually during heat waves in the summer or over a sunny Easter bank holiday to try and help me get in the mood to edit this book.

Thanks to my wonderful agents, Clare and Lydia, for supporting me through this first foray into the world of adult writing and for all your hard work making this happen. And thanks to my editor, Charlotte Ledger, for taking a chance on me!

I don't know whether to thank my family or apologise to them, because honestly, you guys put up with so much from me at Christmas. Whether it's my singing of 'Marley and Marley', showing off my Christmas slippers à la Arthur Christmas, or trying to spread as much festive cheer as Buddy the Elf. Thanks Mum, for always putting so much effort into Christmas, and for making a gorgeous Christmas dinner. Thanks Dad, for that Jingle All The Way-style dash for stockings that one year I'll never forget. Thanks Auntie Sally and Uncle Jason, for the 'driving home for Christmas' mug and for always letting us help decorate the tree. Thanks to Gransha, for always being my biggest fan, and reliably asking for 'just some Mars Bars' at Christmas.

Also, to Auntie Sally and Uncle Jason – it's been eight years since the Great Turkeypocalypse of 2011. I don't think I will ever recover from it. I couldn't resist a reference to it in this book.

This novel focuses on the relationship between two sisters – and to my own sister, thanks for being such a brilliant sister and Baby, It's Cold Outside singalong partner, for putting up with my nonsense. I'm so proud to be your big sister ... Even if I'm dancing around town wearing my Christmas jumper and embarrassing you.

Kudos to the gang at work for helping me balance everything on the writing side alongside my day job – whether it's jetting off to Brazil for a weekend or not finding it weird when I say I've spent my weekend working. A special nod to Barb and Jade for making 'the worst office in the world' the best, and for all your mad stories. Especially the naked volleyball one.

For my friends, thanks for indulging me when I buy you Christmas presents simply because I can't help myself, and for always rooting for me, whatever it is. My Ghana Gals, my Dream Team, my Ovaries of Physics, and my lab buddy Harrison. You guys are the best. Love you forever.